RETAIL STREET FIGHT:

RETAIL SERVICE HAS BEEN CALLED OUT…AND THE GLOVES NEED TO COME OFF!

by

Arnold Capitanelli, III

Snellville, GA
www.customeradvocateprograms.com
An Experience Relationship Programs company

Retail Street Fight

ISBN number: 978-1-59712-358-7

Dedication

This book is lovingly dedicated to my wife and children, who have endured the painstaking process of supporting me through the madness that I have called a career.

Acknowledgment & Gratitude

There are a countless number of people who have touched my life over the years, supported me in my endeavors and mentored me to become who I am today, warts and all. This list is a feeble attempt at remembering all of them. In chronological order:

Mom and Dad – my original business mentors. You taught me that serving was a blessing, not a burden.

The Hanouceks – You guys started it all. You saw the potential in this struggling shoe salesperson and gave me the stage for my first understanding of how to create memorable experiences.

Steve Hammock and Tom Neal – My first exposure to passion, culture and one of the strongest belief systems I have ever been absorbed into.

Harry J. Friedman – You were, are, and will always be a dear friend in my heart. You gave me the platform to build my beliefs.

The Goldrich Family – True retail merchants. Nobody knows this game better than you. You blessed me with reality.

Steven Erlbaum – Thanks for taking a shot on me. You taught me how to trust my gut instincts. You epitomize entrepreneurialism.

Bob Huth – No man has ever done more for me in my education, development, and understanding of relationship selling. Your belief in me was unwavering—even when many would have given up. You are all over this book and I couldn't have written it without you.

Tom Johnson – In the short period of time we worked together, I never learned more about servant leadership. You embody passion. I will forever value our friendship.

Peter Abruzzo - You took me into your arena and showed me how to fight on the streets.

Jake Bell – Your loyalty is unbending.

Tony Howell – Thanks for giving me the strength to gamble on myself.

The Spencer Family – You are the spirit behind this book. The gift of serving others brings me back full circle to the lessons I learned from my own family. You are my family.

Thank you everyone else not mentioned here who believed.

Table of Contents

Foreword:

A Divine Appointment

We will never forget the first time we met Arnie Capitanelli. He first appeared to this group of southern business men as a slick, smooth talking, dressed to the nine's Italian. And he was doing his best to convince us that he can teach us something not only about the customer but also about our organization. To be frank we weren't initially buying what he was selling. It might have been the whole last name thing (could we really trust a guy with a last name like that?). Well, we must have because it wasn't two months later before Arnie was conducting workshops with our management team. He was God's provision for our company at a time when we recognized that we needed to achieve a higher level of sales performance and also enhance the overall customer experience.

Seven short years ago we started a single retail furniture store producing a sales volume of less than $2,000,000. Since then we've grown to a multi-store regional chain with a sales level of $61,000,000. But, in the midst of a slowing economy we were experiencing some challenges and recognized that we needed help. We have heard it said that the first step in solving any problem is to admit one has a problem. We were admitting that we had problems and Arnie's arrival proved to be the solution in which we were looking.

We don't know why difficulties and hard times devastate some companies and at the same time stimulate and revitalize others. In light of this dichotomy, we knew that we needed help and that hard times were definitely ahead. We vividly remember our debate regarding spending capital during these uncertain times to invest in Arnie's services. Should we? Could we? Without a doubt, our decision to forge a relationship with Arnie has been one of the best decisions we have ever made. We felt that leadership development was one of our largest areas for opportunity and growth. At the time we were wrestling with complacency and mere compliance at all levels within our organization and knew that it had to change. Arnie listened to our concerns and answered each leadership development issue by helping us to realize what distinguishes one retailer from the next: the customer experience.

We have often made the statement that when Arnie Capitanelli is in his element there is no one that can touch him. He is a barn burner when it comes to a selling system built on one foundation: the consumer. Arnie understands the complete selling cycle, customer readiness, staff readiness, productive communication, customer experience, gap analysis, coaching, role playing, performance development, customer retention, community and the uncanny ability to communicate and demonstrate at a level that is second to none. What we have appreciated the most about Arnie is that he didn't just come into our organization as a master ninja or black belt communicator, he became a part of our culture in order to help us attain the results we so desired. These results have given us a customer belief system that has become the marrow to our retail bones. It is the source which has breathed life back into our culture and into the customer experience. This belief system is still growing within our company and it constantly wages war against our biggest enemy, compliance. Arnie reveals to us during each visit that if productivity expectations come from compliance it will only achieve nominal results. He has helped us to understand the importance and necessity of sales associates having an internal belief system that embraces our mission and our customer expectation. Our leadership team, with the help of Arnie, has embraced this concept in every facet of our business. The ultimate goal is to make certain that every manager and every sales associate embraces this truth – ***EVERY CUSTOMER COUNTS.***

We are a company that at the foundation is rooted in a system of beliefs outside the consumer experience as well. We believe that our Lord provides and sustains us no matter the circumstances or obstacles that we face in this retail world; a God that knows our needs before we even know that there is a need. God knew that we had a need for Arnie Capitanelli. Arnie, you were truly a divine appointment, one that will always have your texture woven within the fabric of our company.

Many Thanks!!!!!

Jim & Chad Spencer
The Spencer Group
Top 100 Furniture Retailer

Warning

The book you are about to read uses frank and explicit language regarding service in the world of independent retailing. If you are not ready to confront the reality of poor customer experiences; if you think things are just fine in your store; if you feel your merchandising and marketing efforts are enough, this book may not be for you. But if you are sensing that your customer experience could be better, then read on. If you have been grappling with how to compete in an arena where your opponent is bigger and has cooler weapons, then read on. If you're tired, running on shoestring margins, and wondering if there is anything you can do to slay the beast, read on.

The rest of you—read on anyway. Chances are, you're kidding yourself.

The Challenge

"Somewhere north of indifference are eager people who want to do good work but just don't know they're supposed to."

ArnieCAP

Introduction:

The Challenge

Independent and Specialty Retailers around the globe, I'd like you to take pause for a moment and consider the following: if you were asked to define the competitive advantage you have in your marketplace over the mass merchants, category killers, the Internet and catalogs, and TV Shopping Networks that carry the same brands you do, how would you respond? Would you proclaim a higher level of service as something customers get in your store that they can't experience in these other retailing models? If so, then are you completely sure that this perceived edge for maintaining market share and increasing revenue and profitability is actually manifested when customers shop your store? And finally, do you know for sure that your customer base actually experiences a higher-touch service model when interacting with your staff? Does your store "out-serve" the others based on how customers today define customer service?

I believe the claim independent retailers make regarding their perceived service advantage is being called to the streets. And if you think you are going to win this fight based solely on an assumption that your customer experience model is in fact superior, you are sadly mistaken. Your challengers; Big Box Category Killers, the Internet and national catalogs have thrown down the gauntlet. They are using the perception that better pricing, bottomless marketing budgets, brand recognition, deeper margins and systemic processes that create ease of buying defines the "service" people are looking for today.

Over the past decade or so the retail industry and all of the innovators, consultants and efficiency experts that guide our decisions have educated our customer base on how to serve themselves. We have made the need for high-touch, customer-centric relationship selling somewhat of a dinosaur. Even the tech sector has made claim to Customer Relationship Management via systemic outreach programs that manages the shopping/buying behaviors of customers thus usurping the salesperson's mandate to prospect and seek for referrals.

What the independent category specialist needs to know is that selling and serving customers is not an innate perfunctory condition of your business model. Superior service isn't assumed in the fact that you exist as the specialty retail alternative to self serve and virtual shopping. Selling and serving customers must become an active, conscious, methodical initiative of your business model in order for it to be realized or claimed as the competitive advantage you have in your market. Consider this; if you have been in business more than a couple of years there's a good chance your merchandising and marketing strategies most likely follow a model. My guess is those components of your business aren't so random. So does your customer experience have "a model" as well? Do you have a system, a strategy, a defined expectation for how to serve, whom should serve, and measuring the way your staff serves?

Just because you hired people to sell and serve your customers doesn't mean that it's actually happening. The existence of humans in your store to serve and sell doesn't preclude that they are actually serving just because it's part of their title or job description. Selling, serving and delivering superior customer experiences all have to be organized, orchestrated and an obvious dynamic of your business model.

This is a Retail Street Fight and it's not a civilized, organized fight either. The gloves are off. The reality is that brick and mortar retailers have only one move considered to be the dreaded-pretzel hold of this match. This move is fought on the sales floor and it's the one thing you can do that they can't. Now before you come to the conclusion that this is just another metaphorical book about customer service and salesmanship, think again. You all know that your previous attempts to "train" your people to serve and sell better and hold them accountable to performance and selling standards is about as effective, long-term, as an all protein diet. Let's be honest. The old fire in the belly salesperson has gone by the way of the Oldsmobile. And the frustration of trying to get the new generation of retail associates with their texting, instant gratification, and palm up mentality is numbing to the retail operator.

What I'm seeing in brick and mortar retailing today; what we pass off as customer service lacks passion, direction, discipline, consistency and commitment. Today stores seem to be inhabited with human Product Knowledge Kiosks who hope customers will buy if they "do a good demo" or operational robots hiding in task work. And then don't get me started with the "wireless congregator" who gets through their shift, passing the time by talking to their buddies around the store on headsets that their companies provided for them for the purpose of serving customers better.

Category Specialists are hit the hardest with this dynamic. Thankfully they still stand a chance to woo the customer away from portals into the global market place and wholesale clubbing. The category specialists are the retailers with a product category that is singular in assortment (like mattresses) and/or caters to hobbyists and professionals that have a distinct product need. The category specialist sells cameras, musical equipment, bikes and other outdoor or recreational products, soccer stuff, quilting and sewing supplies, jewelry, cigars, running gear, golf and sporting goods, cell phones, records and vintage products, scuba gear, pools and spas, books, etc, etc.

There's a story that I tell when I'm brought in to speak at a convention or private function that is the basis for this book. This story is real and is happening in retail stores around the country every day.

My wife decided one day to upgrade her digital camera to a SLR (single lens reflex). She was frustrated with the time lag from pressing the button to when the picture was taken and the fact that she couldn't take multiple pictures by holding down the shutter button.

So she decided that she would look into a Nikon D-40 and the Cannon Rebel. Initially she did an exhaustive comparison on various Internet sites; an activity that drives me nuts. Then on an unrelated visit, she drifted over to the camera section at our local Big Box mass merchant. After the frustration of attempting to try a product that was tethered to a counter while the sales associate watched, she ventured back to the Internet to do more comparisons.

Finally I pressed her to go to the local camera shop for a real, hands-on product demo. So she did. Off to the local camera store she went while I took the kids to the movies. When I got out of the movie theatre, I noticed her car in the parking lot and went into to see how she was doing. The Human Product Knowledge Kiosk had both cameras out and had done a fabulous job explaining the differences between the two cameras, and thus a decision was made.

"I think I'm gonna get the D-40" she told me privately when I pressed her to make a decision. And so I wrangled up the kids and told her that I would wait for her in the car. About 10 to 15 minutes later she came out…empty handed!

I asked her, "What happened?"

"I'm going to get the D-40," she said.

"Are they making it for you?" I sarcastically replied.

"No, I just thought I would go back on the Internet and find the best price," she informed me.

"Didn't she ask you to buy it?" I said as I felt my blood begin to heat up.

"Not really. She just thanked me, told me her name, and said if I had any more questions she would be happy to help. And…I left."

"You understand," I said with as much reserve as I could muster up, "that if you go home and buy this thing on the Internet, it will invalidate my entire existence!" I advised her to go back into the store and demo the camera again and wait there until the associate asked her to buy it.

About 10 minutes later, I went into the store to see what was taking so long. There they were, with both cameras out again on the counter. Resisting the urge to do a sales seminar, I asked the associate what was happening. She told me that she wasn't sure but it seemed that the D-40 was the right camera. I said, "Did you ask her to buy it?" A far away look appeared on the woman's face. She looked at my wife and asked, "So, do you want this one?" My wife acknowledged and the deal was done.

Can you imagine what it took to make this sale? And of course you know that if I hadn't pressed my wife to go back in and hadn't gone back in myself to urge the associate to close the sale, this would have ended up completely different. Nikon would have been happy that their product was chosen, but the local retailer would have missed out.

Now, I fully believe that this salesperson is not mal-intended, just ill-informed and misdirected. She is clearly not dialed into the company's initiatives relative to customer experiences and making sales. It's that simple. She wasn't trying not to sell; she just didn't know she was supposed to.

So now, you might think that what this store needs is to give their associates sales quotas or goals, performance accountability, train them on closing techniques and maybe even mandate that closing the sale and adding on become policies of the store. The district manager needs a well crafted store action plan with smart goals. There needs to be consequences for non-compliance.

Well, guess what. In the early 90s, they tried that. The Camera Store in this story actually instituted such a program. I know…I was the one who delivered it. The program developed for them, nearly 20 years ago, is now virtually non-existent today. To be fair, much has happened in the past 20 years and I'm not suggesting that the program was at fault or ineffective. It's just that it had no sustainability. It was a bolt on, feel good, apple pie training moment. It was like dropping an Alka Seltzer in a glass of water; a lot of initial activity, but after awhile, the fizz goes away and we're back to a still glass of water with a lot of ineffective particles floating around in it. The primary reason the program dissolved was that as the program was being delivered and implemented it was viewed by the store and field operators as an exercise in compliance. It never became a shared belief system within the organization from the very people who paid to have the program implemented—the owner and his senior team.

If you are in your office right now, turn around and look at your bookshelf. Do you see all the books, videos, seminar manuals and programs you've attempted to implement in your company? Chances are, there are quite a few, and chances are, they have become nothing more than iconic reminders of what you hoped would have become the program that would improve the way your associates behaved when serving your customers. These programs are like toupees. Everyone makes fun of them until one is needed. But, like the toupee, these programs just cover up a symptom of a much deeper problem and never actually turn out as hoped.

This is retail, folks. We're selling stuff people want. Sure, it is essential that salespeople know how to ask a customer to buy and that certain items with higher margins should be offered early and often. Sales goals, performance metrics and closing techniques are foundational to selling, but aren't nearly as effective as when the company creates an awareness of the value of every single customer within the very people who serve them. In fact, a company is better off with a strong belief about service with no technique than with a lot of technique and no shared belief system.

The independent specialty retailer is the backbone of its respective industries. Service is our only advantage. The choice is simple:

Become an efficient, lean machine
and try to fight on their street
Or
Become a high touch provider and reclaim your street.

If the people working in your store don't have a shared belief about what it means when that door swings, then all the aforementioned necessities of retailing are the proverbial three–legged stool.

I don't know if you're like me, but I refuse to buy anything on the Internet unless I cannot find it locally. And I don't just shop the independents; I'll shop the local big-box and the large multi-unit chains as well. Because even though the revenue is going back to Columbus or Philly or Washington, the local store employs my neighbors and pays local taxes. I want to be part of the solution, not the problem. I was nauseated one day when the weatherman on the local NBC affiliate commented one Christmas season that he can't take the crowds during the season and does all his shopping on the Internet. Can you imagine how the show's sponsors felt having spent the money to advertise that morning only to have the weatherman poo-poo brick and mortar shopping?

It's time for retailers to recognize that we need to have a compelling reason for customers to shop and buy in our stores. Its time for consumers to reclaim their retail stores and demand that their expectations be met and provide them with a shopping experience that cannot be replicated online, over a catalog phone line, or on a television shopping network.

This book is for you if you think your staff can deliver better customer experiences. This book is for you if your retail model attracts employees who love to talk about your product, but aren't inclined to want to sound "salesman-y". This book is for you if you're tired of whining about how to compete against price and marketing. This book is for you if you want to learn the dreaded-pretzel hold of retailing; the one move you have that can keep the locals coming to your store.

This book is for the street-wise fighter who doesn't have the patience to learn complicated selling systems and can't afford to lose people by using high-compliance methods for getting associates to behave properly.

If you own, operate or manage a retail store of any consequence, this book is for you. I walked these streets with you. I fought this fight. I've worked for the indie, the chain and the category killer and I know what it takes to salvage the independent retailer's shrinking customer base. This book is not philosophical, but it's not tactical either; it's fundamental. This book recognizes that the people who work for you are self-intended and your desires to get them to "buy-in" and think like an owner is not realistic. This book shows you how to get people to tap into their innate nature to be personable, hospitable and solution oriented.

So rip off the tape and throw down your gloves. This is going to be a street fight, and it'll be fought on your street. You may be the underdog—but this is a fight you can win.

Pre-Fight

"Management is not entitlement. It is a commitment to uphold the values, the beliefs and the service culture of the company. It is an agreement to serve the company in a way that maximizes each customer experience and promotes a healthy, thriving and profitable business."

ArnieCAP

Chapter 1:

Pre-Fight

I know it's cliché to say that this book was a labor of love, but the fact is that the lessons and insights represented here is a culmination of the experiences of my life serving retail customers. It's hard to believe that when I look back over the past 25 years of my life, I began my career walking door-to-door in Hackensack, N.J., peddling Electrolux vacuum cleaners. I had no formal education, or direction for that matter. But I did know this: I really liked selling. And it wasn't selling so much that turned me on; I actually didn't want to associate myself with some of the stereotypical attributes that one would classify as "salesperson". It was the side benefits—the stage, the feeling of developing relationships, the impressions I could make, the accolades, my freedom to charm and innocently flirt. Most of all, it was the feeling I got when I knew I had served someone beyond their expectations. When they said, "I'll take it," I didn't immediately count the commissions or mentally pump my fist over the win; I was reveling in the moment that my customer found something that they truly wanted, needed, desired. That is what I celebrated. And this book is about celebrating the presence of a customer in our brick and mortar retail establishments.

Over these past 25 years, I sold vacuums, hot tubs, industrial supplies, shoes and apparel, musical instruments, and consulted across a dozen other categories. But it wasn't until I came across a product that I would have never dreamed would be the one that changed the way I looked at serving and salesmanship. The product was the wedding gown and the company that taught me these valuable lessons was David's Bridal.

Here's what I know to be true: it doesn't matter whether you run a small, family-owned business or you're the president of a large organization consisting of multiple brands. There is one primary objective for sustaining performance and building lasting relationships with your customers; get the front line organization to deliver superior experiences consistently with every customer that enters your store. If you are a company of any size or substance, I hope, no I pray, that you fully understand that your primary objective is to serve people. I didn't say service people, or provide service, or deliver great customer service— I said, "serve people". Cars get serviced, people are served. So serve them beyond their expectations. After all, what else does the independent retailer have?

That perspective on retailing never became more clear to me when in 1998 I heard the most profound, the most visionary brand statement of my entire career; a 25-year career of working and consulting for some of the brightest stars in retail.

This book begins with the end in mind. In January of 1998, I began working for David's Bridal, which had about 55 stores at the time. Early in my tenure with the company I sat in an executive staff meeting where I heard this most profound statement—the one that changed my perspective on retail sales and performance management forever. One of the marketing executives asked the CEO what he thought would be the fulcrum of the company's success. His reply created a painfully pregnant pause among the merchants and marketers in the room who thought for sure that the value messaging or the incomparable assortment would surely be the core ingredient for our growth. In sharp contrast to what was thought to be the unique advantage David's Bridal had was this fertile statement. Are you ready? The response was…

"We will serve the underserved."

I'd like you to read that statement a few times and let the potency of its meaning seep into the fabric of what you believe to be your mission statement or corporate culture. "We'll serve the underserved." Generally speaking, retail service in America is declining, or at the very least is predictable and rote. We are in the throws of a denigration of first and second generation businesses. Brick and mortar retailers are reaching levels of apathy never experienced before.

And the lack of passionate service has resulted in customers believing they are better off serving themselves. That's one of the reasons why the Internet is so appealing as well as self-serve environments. This is where you can compete. This is where the fight can be won; because while the IT geeks and the supply chain gurus are trying to use CRM software and efficiency to woo the customer to them, you have human-to-human contact as your secret weapon.

Let me share with you what that statement meant to the growth of David's Bridal and how it single-handedly changed an industry. Before David's, if you were a recently engaged women who was beginning the process of shopping for a wedding gown, chances were that the only way you would truly see how the gown you had been dreaming about since you were three years old was going to look was if the bridal salon had a sample of the dress in your size. If not, the salon consultants went into a fanciful dance of pinning, hanging and fluffing a garment in a way to give you an idea of what it looked like. Then if you liked it, you were most likely required to pay for it in full and wait for it to be ordered.

If you were not blessed with sample sizing, if you and your fiancé were bearing the cost of the wedding without parental assistance, or you just wanted to take the gown home today and look at it in your own mirror with your friends, then the experience for procuring the item central to the most important day of your life was painful, drawn out and quite expensive. David's Bridal saw this as an opportunity to "serve the underserved".

A bride who was required to mold her expectations around the service and assortment of the local bridal salon would now be able to have an experience where she would be assisted by associates who embraced the company's belief about serving the underserved. She would try on gowns in her size. The gown would be made of luxurious fabrics and styling yet priced at a tremendous value. And the assortment would allow that bride to take her gown home… today! An experience that well exceeded her expectations.

If you are a retail executive in any department and make decisions that directly impact the customer experience (which are 99 percent of your decisions), then I believe it is your mandate to begin each decision making process with that statement.

Delivering superior customer experiences may sound to you like a simplistic, almost idealistic statement, and it is often assumed by senior management that field leaders are driving this message. But the reality is that this is often not the case. In fact, accomplishing this objective is often derailed by a field team that gets trapped in a vicious cycle of chasing the tangible, operational dynamics of their stores as opposed to ensuring that each customer is served consistently and beyond their expectations. They believe this to be the true objective of their job responsibilities because they are ultimately held accountable for operational integrity and merchandising compliance. I put emphasis on the word "believe" because I have come to learn that it is the best word to describe what fuel's a person's behaviors and decision-making.

I have interviewed more than one man's share of store, district and regional management. And almost without fail, each one of them has professed in their interview that having service standards and holding people accountable for customer service was critical to their success. But dig a little about the objective and "tone" of their store visits and you will uncover their personal "core beliefs" regarding store performance and behavioral accountability. Or better yet, just shop one of their stores and you will experience for yourself the store's core beliefs about customer experiences and what they believe their field superiors expect from them. You will typically find these associates are either focused on operational action plans and activities, or they are behaving in a way in line with their own beliefs, which often is counter to the company's expectations for service delivery.

Most field supervisors I have interviewed and worked with through the years are much more prone to conducting store visits based on operational compliance and pushing performance metrics for the sake of the metric and not for the true objective which is to deliver superior customer experiences. Their company credo or mission statement may stress customer service, but their core belief system about what is important, what decisions need to be made, and the behaviors that come from those decisions are often askew from the company's desire to serve customers beyond their expectations.

Many of these interviews were with field leaders from well known, mall-based and strip center chains. I have often walked away from the interview thinking that the interviewee was completely out of touch with the reality of service in their stores. The service dynamics they describe in these interviews are nearly non-existent when I shop these stores with my family. In most cases, the employees in these stores are either caught up in operational or merchandising tasks, are self-absorbed with personal issues or completely lack any sense of outgoingness or passion for serving others. In many cases, one would think that they either don't like engaging with people they have no pre-existing relationship with, or they are disenchanted with the prospect of serving other people as a way to earn a living. This is usually because the service standards the DM is driving are based on a compliance system as opposed to a belief system; in other words, "behavior is required, not desired". Or the supervisor is hoping that camaraderie, informality and friendship will drive behavioral compliance.

What I see in retail today is this:

- When compliance becomes the foundation for service delivery, the associate engages in a game of "what can I get away with when the supervisor is not around".

- When camaraderie is the method, the associates think it's suggestive.

- When a belief system is the foundation for service delivery, the sales associate can find the right behaviors by tapping into a shared understanding about why the customer experience is a priority.

- When the beliefs drive the service model and the disciplines for serving customers are known, then an associate will enlist the right behaviors from an internal trigger rather than from some degree of obedience or affinity for the supervisor.

This point of view for running a customer-centric business model flies in the face of some tried and true old-school methods. Quite frankly, I cut my teeth on a very successful program based on performance and behavioral accountability. This format has been an integral part of the performance management model of many retailers and sales organizations over the years. And I'm not suggesting in any way that there shouldn't be performance expectations for staff or behavioral standards for that matter. But there's a new generation in the sales force and they are more self-intended than ever before. Holding a retail salesperson to a tight-rope of performance compliance today is increasingly more difficult than ever before. Even with unemployment at pinnacle levels maintaining a stable staff eager to serve the customer and the company's profits is the biggest constraint in retail today.

I've been speaking on this subject for nearly 20 years and have developed customer centric sales and performance management models for several well-known companies. The one thing I run into the most is the anxiety store managers experience trying to hold sales people highly accountable to a compliance-based customer service model and the frustration when "their friends won't respect their authority".

Front-line managers truly struggle with this. They struggle with the skill-set for coaching people, the confrontation, the opinion leaders who control the sales-floor, the mutiny when its time to role-play; the whole shebang. And then, the one thing I see more than anything else is that managers are so operationally burdened and payroll strapped that the idea of calling someone out on a compliance issue shy of stealing is about the last thing they want to tackle.

Retail is an interesting industry. The financial community takes a very serious look at the revenue performance and profitability of retail companies. Because, at the end of the day, if the numbers dictate that a company is performing, they don't care so much about the particulars. The lack of sense in that is that poor customer experience is a precursor to future poor performance. Yet, the very people who are most responsible for ensuring that customers are happy with their experiences and that cash registers ring are generally inexperienced and uninspired to serve consumers to a degree that exceeds their shopping expectations.

This is an interesting phenomenon. Would you be likely to invest in a tech stock if the development team had no formal training on how to write code? How inclined would you be to invest in a pharmaceutical company if the developers of prescription drugs never took a course in chemistry? Yet we find people investing in retail companies that hire salespeople who have never even read a book on service excellence and managers who never took a basic business course or received training on how to recruit, hire and develop associates to deliver the company's customer experience expectations.

Although the corporate vision and mission emphasizes exceeding a customer's experience as a core value of the brand, it is more likely that real estate, marketing, and the assortment consume a company's key initiatives. Service then becomes a necessary dynamic because customers need to be "processed" through the brand, but often the corporate organization sees the field organization as a necessary evil as opposed to the carrier of the torch.

But here is the greatest paradox of all—the people who are most likely to make up the sales force of typical specialty retailers are also the demographic that makes most shopping decisions. They're the demographic spending cash day in and day out at their local mall or shopping center. And if they don't like being poorly served or aggressively sold when they're shopping, they will likely engage a counter-productive service model of avoidance. This fact is not to be underestimated. When was the last time you interviewed a potential sales associate and asked, "Tell me about you as a customer? How do you like to be served?" What will be revealed are the candidate's beliefs about engaging and serving the customers in your store.

Most customer experiences in retail today are mediocre and lack a certain degree of empathy; meaning a certain understanding of what a customer wants in terms of being served. As a result, the retail paradigm evolved to one of self-service and relies on the use of technology, communications, supply chain efficiencies, etc. to aid in a customer's ability to serve herself. We now have a new model of customer service and it's called self-serve. High-touch has evolved into high-tech and customer centricity has evolved into process efficiency. The self-serve check out lane at the grocery store has a computerized voice that will thank you for your purchase. The human standing at the podium to ensure no one is jacking a 12-pack of sodas will seldom blink your way.

One would think that front line associates would be inclined to use the golden rule as a baseline for serving and selling. But this is not always the case. The truth is that the golden rule is not adequate enough to create a belief system in the sales associate for how to deliver great customer experiences consistently. The things that people do everyday; the way they behave is driven by a set of core values, beliefs, and rationale; not by compliance and performance accountability or by some caffeinated pump-up session designed to motivate and inspire behavioral consistency. Simply put, their personal beliefs drive their day-to-day behaviors when serving customers, not checklists and rote action plans that their DM delivered. And truth be known that compliance and performance accountability is moot when there is a plethora of retail jobs available for similar pay in every mall and strip center in the country.

Let me give you an example of behavior being driven by a "belief system". One day when flying back east on a red-eye from Los Angeles, a mother and small child were on my flight and unfortunately designated to middle seats of different rows on the plane. One of the middle seats was next to a business traveler across the aisle from me. When the flight attendant asked this gentleman to give up his seat to accommodate the mother and child, he refused. This request would have caused him to have to give up an aisle seat for a middle seat on a coast-to-coast, red-eye flight. The gentleman in this situation made a decision based on his core beliefs and behaved accordingly, based on the fact that he perceived no real consequences for not complying with the request.

Now, the question is, if the traveler's minister, parents or own wife and child had been present, would he have complied with the request? My guess is "yes," not because of his core beliefs, but because at that moment he would have been under the scrutiny of someone who would have judged him and held him accountable for his behavior. But when left to his own devices, his true belief system emerged.

What if the mother and child who were separated on this flight were his own wife and child? Would he have chastised a fellow traveler for not accommodating them? Probably so…so much for the golden rule!

Having witnessed this situation, I offered my aisle seat up to the business traveler, which in turn freed up two adjacent seats for the mother and child, and I took the mother's original middle seat. Why would I do this? It's certainly not because I'm a martyr or thought it would make a great story for a book. I behaved in a way that aligned with my values. My core beliefs could not fathom the idea that this mother and child would have to travel for five hours through the night separated by several rows; not to mention the other travelers who would have to sit within proximity of a child separated from his mother through the night.

Empathy drives my decisions and behaviors; it is a central attribute of my core beliefs. This is who I am.

Allow me to take this scenario down to earth and provide a more common example of how a person's beliefs drive their behaviors in a way that is counter to their company's customer experience expectations. One night I was traveling through Wisconsin with two district managers who worked for me in Chicago, Jake Bell and Raji Shah, true retail street fighters. Their core beliefs and innate passion to ensure customers were being served allowed me as their supervisor to lead and develop them as opposed to manage them.

We were on our way to an industry show when we stopped for dinner at a popular steakhouse chain. The restaurant had a huge yellow banner hanging outside advertising their gift card program for the holidays. After a nice dinner, some laughs, and lengthy banter about salesmanship and our shared vision for improving the service delivery of our market, our server brought the bill. As I scanned the bill and reached for my credit card, the server said; "I have to ask if you would be interested in purchasing a gift card for the holidays." Obviously, this revelation of the server's beliefs struck a chord at the very soul of everything I personally believe in. "You have to ask?" I replied. The server replied; "Yes," and continued to explain that it was a requirement and they had gone through training on how to offer the program. I asked the server how he felt about offering the gift card and his reply opened a window into his core belief system that quite frankly could have been uncovered in the most rudimentary of job interviews.

In a nutshell, he flat out proclaimed that he did not believe his customers were really very interested in restaurant gift cards. This was driven by his personal belief. Because he found no value in it, his customers would most likely feel the same way as well.

I probed deeper into the server's beliefs. Why would he behave in a way that was counter to the company's expectations? It turns out that the server has a belief system that would be more in line with non-profit organizations. His desires for his own future would cause him to ultimately seek out a career in social work. He is serving tables at this point in his life because he's working his way through college. I certainly have no problem with his personal aspirations. I have a great respect for people and companies who provide services and help mankind in a not-for-profit business model. What I take issue with is that the server accepted employment from a company whose business model requires profitability. He didn't mind serving others to make his living but he was disconnected with the company's goal of driving top line and bottom line results. His belief system is counter-productive to the company's profit goals and what the company's executives believe their customers want.

This scenario begs the following questions be asked:

- If the server's belief system had been uncovered in an interview, should the company have hired him?

- Could the company have learned underneath the surface of his work experience what they needed to know about the server in order to better understand his personal beliefs and how they would shape his behaviors when serving customers?

- Could they have tapped into his belief system as a way to cause him to offer the gift card program without feeling like he was negotiating his personal values?

The answer to all these questions is yes, provided the server comes to the party with a passion to serve, an outgoingness to engage with total strangers quickly and with a sense of pride, and an understanding of his obligations and responsibilities of the job he was interviewing for. And yes, the "program" that facilitates this is tangible, can be replicated, and can be taught (I use the word taught instead of trained because of the implications of learning vs. complying).

So what actually is a belief system? Is it something you are born with and is part of your being throughout your life? Or can it develop, grow and evolve as you meet people who influence your thoughts and decisions as you go through life? In the chapter "You Gotta Believe," there will be a deeper look into how to develop a belief system for your company based on knowing what customers expect from your service model. Some basic core beliefs will be provided to give a starting place by which you can build your own belief system. The book will also show you how to incorporate them into your customer experience.

Ultimately what I intend for this book is to provide the weapons needed for those interested in taking on this fight. Retailers from all walks of life and industries will learn how to break beyond the antiquated methods of managing people through compliance and fear or attempting to stress the importance of serving others using camaraderie. I will provide a detailed accounting of how my belief system was developed and the influences in my life that molded it. I will outline methods for motivating front line associates responsible for serving and delivering superior experiences through the development of a belief system and tapping into the passion they should have when doing so. Each chapter is a distinct weapon that will make the fight against the 800-pound gorilla a fair fight. This book is a fundamental format for how to deliver superior customer experiences consistently regardless of your service model and gives the Internet and category killers a run for the customer's loyalty.

The content of this book comes from a training program I developed for independent retailers called "Every Customer Counts—A Customer Advocate Program". The program, also known as CAP, is built on a five pillar concept created to focus a retail organization on customer centric-activities that maximizes the potential of each transaction and exposes erosion in the disciplines that define a superior customer experience.

The program is laid out as:

1. Foundations for Customer Centricity: Defining and implementing beliefs systems, organizational disciplines and performance accountabilities that form the foundation for success.

2. The Customer Experience - Made Simple: The creation of specific disciplines, techniques and training tools that underlie the customer experience and ensure store teams can deliver those experiences with each customer. A retailer's selling and service delivery model must promote relationship building with customers.

3. Gap Analysis – Minimizing Performance Erosion: Tracking individual and actionable performance indicators that provide direction on how to improve customer experiences.

4. Being the Customer Advocate: Evolving from antiquated traditional models of sales management to being an advocate for each customer's experience. Developing the skills managers need to have in order to ensure the core values of beliefs, disciplines, awareness and commitment are being demonstrated with every customer interaction.

5. Staffing The Experience: Recruiting people who are passionate about selling and serving and then developing their desire to serve others using sustainable learning systems as opposed to compliance based training programs. Learning

platforms ensure that anyone who interacts with the customer is representing the company's beliefs and exceeding customer expectations.

The foundation of the program is steeped with market research and customer feedback. The program identifies the ways an independent retail store can build both Market Penetration (transactions) and Customer Share (average transaction) by capitalizing on critical moments in the customer experience.

The key to CAP's success however lies in the method in which it moves salespeople to behave in a way that exceeds customer expectations and maximizes each customer facing opportunity. CAP is built on these basic tenets:

1. Every customer counts. Success in retail begins with an awareness of the importance of every single footprint. In today's marketplace, the presence of a customer in a brick and mortar retail store is not happenstance.

2. Salespeople are generally self-intended; they will typically default to behavior based on what they believe is right for them. Therefore performance management models that lean to the extremes of either high compliance or high camaraderie will not have a long-term effect on behavior. In order to create and sustain behavioral consistency, the associate's core beliefs must be addressed.

3. Goal setting should be motivating, inspiring, and based on personal levels of achievement. Goal setting is ineffective when used to punish or humiliate. Performance accountability, on the other hand, is based on defined minimum contribution benchmarks. Feedback on individual performance is reserved for performance improvement meetings.

4. Gaps in the customer experience are realized in performance trends of actionable metrics. If the associate is not serv-

ing or selling the "correct way" it will show up in a statistical trend.

5. Training creates short-term compliance. Learning creates long-term behavioral change. The employees' experience will shape the customer experience.

Before we close this chapter, I'd like to expose you to what I believe should become the new vocabulary in retail. I happen to be a stickler on words; mostly the intent behind the word being used. I feel some retail nomenclature exists because it has always been that way. But it's time for us to really examine what it is we are trying to say, the meaning behind the word and the intent it has within the context of how it's being used. The words below will be used frequently in this book and so you may need to refer back to these pages if clarification is needed.

Training becomes Learning
Animals are trained. They are drilled on a behavior in the hopes that there will be a small morsel if done properly. They don't know why they do it, they are responding to the consequence. Humans do best when learning takes place. Training creates short-term compliance; learning enables long term behavioral change.

Selling Standards become Experience Disciplines
Policies are for operational integrity not for the fluid exchange of words between a customer and a salesperson. Selling requires a disciplined approach to serving customers with the goal of exceeding their expectations.

Conversion Rate becomes Market Penetration

Conversion Rate is a ratio of the number of customers who bought to the total number of people shopping. But it does not provide insight to whether the store is penetrating the market by building new customers on top of the existing customer base. Market Penetration is like a compounded interest rate. Advertising's job is to get new customers into the store. Salespeople are required to maintain those relationships. Otherwise marketing dollars are being wasted on customers who should remain loyal to the brand as a result of relationship maintenance not new promotions.

Average Sale becomes Customer Share

Selling to an individual customer requires maximizing the amount of money a customer will spend shopping for a particular need; the share of that customer's budget. If a customer purchased furniture at an Ashley HomeStore and then later picked up accessory items at Pier 1, then the salesperson at Ashley compromised the Customer Share by not attempting to accessorize the purchase during the initial visit or through follow up with that customer. I've met many top performing salespeople with low average sale and high conversion rates. This is an indicator of maximizing Customer Share. The low average sale is driven by repeat customers who are loyal to the brand because the salesperson regularly reaches out to customers when merchandise comes in that coordinates with previous purchases.

Sales Manager becomes Customer Advocate

Store supervisors must develop a sense for how the customer experiences the store. It's no longer just about helping Fred close a sale or regurgitating weekly performance objectives in the hopes that it will boost business. A customer advocate ensures each experience is occurring to the degree that it maximizes the opportunity and creates repeat business by exceeding customer expectations.

Compliance becomes Behavioral Consistency

As you will read in subsequent chapters, I have very strong feelings that a compliance message creates a negative image about management; portraying them as police or dictators. Although it's your store and you should run it the way you want, the goal is to drive consistency as opposed to demand compliance.

Role-playing becomes Scrimmaging

Salespeople hate role-playing. Some managers use the term "skill development" as the alternative. But in an industry that is performance based and tracks individual metrics for the sake of finding behavioral gaps, then sports is the perfect metaphor. Professional athletes, who make millions of dollars, scrimmage to develop the disciplines they need to perform at higher levels.

Opening the Sale becomes Engaging the Customer

Once you realize that "relationship" is foundational for a superior customer experience then the term "Opening the Sale" doesn't make sense. Relationships begin when communication occurs. With that in mind, then the first step or objective when a salesperson decides to approach a customer is to engage the customer.

Probing/Qualifying becomes Discovery

Probing is something that one person does to another. In a relationship, two people are working together for a common goal. Discovery is the process by which a customer and salesperson work together to uncover the motivators causing the customer to seek out products you sell.

The Demonstration/Presentation becomes The Reveal

If you have ever watch a TV show that highlights a designer helping a hopeless homeowner transform a house or specific room, then you have witnessed what show producers call "the reveal". After a thorough amount of discovery, the designer transforms the room based on what was learned. At the show's conclusion, the couple is brought into their transformed room. The reaction of the couple (called "the reveal") is typically overwhelming and filled with emotion. The designer provides little to no explanation of what occurred, because it mirrors what was learned during the discovery period. After taking it in, minor nuances are pointed out that may not be so obvious at first blush. But one thing you never hear from the home owner…"No, that's not exactly what I had in mind."

Goals become Base Contribution Rate

Goals are a very personal thing. They differ from person to person. Goal setting is not an accountability platform. Goal setting should inspire and drive people to perform at higher levels. Base contribution rate is the minimum performance trend or aggregate. There will be more on this in the chapter on Awareness

Progressive Discipline becomes Corrective Action

Similar to compliance, Progressive Discipline conjures up images of harsh consequences that intend to scare an associate into behavioral submission. Corrective Action is the means by which a manager assists an associate to develop the skills necessary to improve performance.

Human Resources becomes Employee Experiences

I don't actually believe I'll be able to change this one, but for the sake of this section I do believe companies must be concerned with how their associates experience the company. Better employee experiences translate into better customer experiences.

So that's my list. Semantics? Maybe. But appreciate the idea that it may be time to rethink exactly what the intent is behind some of the terminology being used today. I put the list on the last page of this chapter so you can rip it out of the book and post it for future reference.

The next chapter is part foundational, part cultural. It addresses the subject of passion. Have you ever had a conversation with someone and in the middle of it touch on a subject that clearly hit a nerve in the person? It's pretty obvious that when someone is passionate about something, it changes the tone of their voice, their body language, their energy, etc. Passion is something that the experts claim is the difference between having a job and having a mission. Passion turns behavior into action. Passion turns visions into reality.

I hope you enjoy reading about how to win the Retail Street Fight as much as I did experiencing it under the guidance of my belief system mentors.

You kiss your Mom with that mouth?
The New Language of Retail

Becomes

Training	Learning
Selling Standards	Experience Disciplines
Average Sale	Customer Share
Conversion Rate	Market Penetration
Sales Manager	Customer Advocate
Compliance	Behavioral Consistency
Role-Playing	Scrimmaging
Opening the Sale	Engaging the Customer
Probing/Qualifying	Discovery
Demonstrations	The Reveal
Goal Setting	Base Contribution Rate
Progressive Discipline	Corrective Action
Human Resources	Employee Experience

Passion –
The Soul of
the Retail Street
Fighter

"Passion ignites desire. It causes people to go beyond their perceived limitations."

ArnieCAP

Chapter 2:

Passion – The Soul of the Retail Street Fighter

This chapter serves as both the beginning of the story and acknowledgment of the people whom I have met in my life and taught me great life lessons. Although I start this chapter in 1987 when I first realized that I had a passion for serving, I cannot dismiss the lessons I learned growing up as one of six Capitanelli children. My parents, Arnold Jr. and Giacomina live their lives serving and giving to others. My family has experienced the highs and lows of prosperity, and regardless of their personal circumstances and varying degrees of fortune, they've always been known as "servers". Ask anyone who knew my parents back in the '70s and '80s when prosperity came to us like shooting fish in a barrel. Ask anyone who knows them now living a comfortable, but modest life as a result of pursuing servitude in their community—and having walked away from most of what was acquired in the early years. Regardless of the decade and the size and value of their portfolio, people who have experienced my parents will undoubtedly use adjectives that describe them as having a passion for serving others. The story associated with the genesis of my core beliefs as a Capitanelli and my passion to serve will make for another book to write as the prequel to this one.

So let's begin. I must go on record as saying that I do not believe there is anything revolutionary in this book. If you are hoping that this book has the newest techniques for closing more sales, you are going to be let down. Here's why:

Every month I religiously buy two magazines; Men's Health and Golf Digest. These magazines promise every month that they now have the secret to six-pack abs and curing my slice. I scour the pages believing that this month the secret will be revealed. Sadly, I still have more flab than ab and my golf ball is sliced more than a tomato facing a Ginsu knife. The reality is that fundamentally there are some basic laws that must be in play for both of these objectives to be realized. For my gut, I must burn more calories than I consume and exercise the muscle. For golf, I have to turn over the club face after making ball-first contact. Everything else, new and old, revolve around those pre-existing principles.

Retailing is no different. And like golf and exercise, it often just requires revisiting the basics, peppered with some new and thought provoking insights. This book is that. It is a culmination and realization of existing truths I have learned throughout my career coupled with some new methods for accomplishing the objective of elevating service.

This chapter addresses my passion as it influenced my professional life and those business mentors who were instrumental in defining my belief system and developing my passion to serve.

The Passion to Serve:

Deliver an experience based on how you want someone to feel.

If you think about people our society has deemed or labeled as icons within their respective field, one could certainly argue that a common thread attribute each had was passion. From Michael Jordon to Mother Teresa, from Bill Gates to Tina Turner; you would be hard pressed to not believe that these people fueled their accomplishments with passion. Many lesser known people may have been as skillful or knowledgeable or talented or resourceful as these people. But the passion these individuals have is arguably a core component of their success, notoriety and rise to the top.

Now I don't profess to be the Michael Jordon of the sales floor or the Mother Teresa of customer service, but as I look back over the past two decades of my life, I can identify critical moments where passion fueled my personal achievements and professional milestones. The first step in the journey was recognizing and tapping into my desire to make memorable impressions on complete strangers. I consider this to be one of the more important ingredients of my career. I wanted the customers who were relying on me to provide them with a product, service or experience to be served beyond their expectations. Did I let people down along the way? Sure I did. Sometimes their expectations were above my abilities; sometimes I fell short of my own expectations. But from a very early age, I knew that if someone was spending money to purchase a product or service, I wanted to make sure the experience attached to it was memorable.

In the mid-80s, having worked in random retail stores in local malls since graduating high school, I found myself selling shoes at a department store called Bullocks in Palm Desert, Calif. My career desires at that time were for the entertainment industry. I was writing and performing music and acting in local theater productions all while working retail during the day. So although at that time I had no belief system tied to a particular company or product I was selling, I did have a passion for engaging with people. I loved it— the schmoozing, the flirting and the exchange of clever quips if I had met a challenger of my quick wittedness. The retail sales floor was my stage and I imagined that with each shoe sale I had the opportunity to make a strong enough impression that the customer might remember me later on when my album broke or my movie was released. "Hey, I bought a pair of shoes from that guy two years ago!" was my motivation and it kept me passionate on the sales floor during those years. Day in and day out I stepped onto the sales floor with the self-intended drive to serve customers. Regardless of my personal circumstances and moments of frustration that my music wasn't turning heads, I knew that I could not let that get in the way of serving and selling to make a living. Truth is…I had a family to support.

One day a white-bearded man and his lovely wife came into my shoe department. To me, the situation was nothing more than another opportunity to sell some shoes and create a memorable impression. What I didn't know was that Bill and Gladys Hanoucek were about to flip the tables on me and create a moment in my life that I would remember forever. Gladys was looking for a pair of shoes; Bill was in need of an outgoing salesperson that could make a dent in his struggling hot tub retail store. Although he had quite a successful master pool business, the retailing of hot tubs was not performing as he had hoped.

Bill was taken by my passion for serving and quickly asked me if I ever thought about making the leap to selling higher ticket items. Initially the thought of pedaling hot tubs did not seem appealing. I masked it with a reply that suggested my lack of product knowledge would make it difficult for me to earn money right out of the gate. I told Bill that it would take too long for me to learn how to sell hot tubs and I couldn't afford the ramp up time to make enough money to provide for my family.

But what Bill knew then, that I would learn later on in life was that product knowledge can be learned, but passion is something you have to bring to the party yourself. My lack of knowledge was not a handicap because Bill knew that salespeople who used product knowledge as a way to show-off their expertise often confused consumers. His mantra was an old selling adage—sell the sizzle, not the steak.

For example, oftentimes customers would come into the store and ask what the horsepower was of the jet pump in a particular hot tub. Initially I had no idea. But what I did know was that people were generally looking for very strong and penetrating jet action. So rather than answering the question directly and trying to fake my way through a technical reply, I walked the customer over to a filled hot tub, turned on the jets, and asked him to feel the action. The facial reaction answered the question and suddenly the request for product information gave way to a term I call the buyer's personal motivator (BPM)—which is the real reason he asked the question. This is where I learned that people don't always ask for what they really want. They translate their BPM into a feature they believe will satisfy their needs. We'll talk more about BPMs in a later chapter in a step called "the reveal," where shopper "wants" and product "haves" join hands.

Bill knew that it was this kind of experience that would sell hot tubs in his store. By the end of the year, I had nearly doubled the amount of spas sold the previous year by a salesman who had been in the hot tub business for many years.

The line of hot tubs I sold when all this started is called HotSpring Portable Spas by Watkins Manufacturing. Although this has been insignificant to the story up to this point, the truth is that the people at Watkins played a pivotal role in my understanding of how a belief system can mold the behaviors of the people whom work within that system. My first exposure to a belief system was when I met the owners and senior executives of Watkins Manufacturing.

O.T. Neil, his son Tom, and Steve Hammock are three of the most passionate people I have ever met. These guys are street fighters. They're driven, passionate, disciplined and one couldn't help but get caught up in the magic they were creating. When they put a team together, they accepted nothing less than a street fighter attitude. In fact, when I interviewed for the job of regional sales manager, one of the first questions asked of me was what college I went to. My response, "Tom, I didn't go to college and if that's what you're looking for, then I'm not the guy. But if you want someone who cut his teeth on the streets of retail; if you want someone who knows how to roll up his sleeves and get on the floor and sell, then look no further." The interview was over and the position was mine.

Watkins would accept nothing less than passion and drive from the team of regional sales managers they put together. They spoke about this line of hot tubs like a group of proud parents. This product wasn't just a vat of hot water that bubbled. It was born of genius—the best materials, superior hydrotherapy and energy efficiency. These gentlemen were so passionate about this product that you wondered if they thought its creation rivaled that of the Internet.

When I met these gentlemen on a tour of the manufacturing facility, it was clear at the onset that the customer was the focus of every company initiative and product design. Tours I had been on with other hot tub companies focused on plant efficiencies, material and labor costs and discounts for truckload purchases. At Watkins, it was about comfort, value and improving people's health and well-being. And if I'm painting a picture of a group of Birkenstock wearing, tree-huggers as the operators of this company—then allow me to color correct. These gentlemen were hungry young businessmen who were driven to succeed.

I joined this company in January of 1988. Immediately they immersed me in the culture of the company. I cut my hair, I traded in my double-breasted suits for blue blazers and gray trousers, and I even tried chewing tobacco. Their passion and belief system was so strong and compelling that I couldn't help but be absorbed into it. By the way, this didn't just happen to me, its not that I'm weak-minded and easily taken in by a cult-like movement. This happened to just about everyone who joined the company. The reason was because you wanted to be a part of the "party" that these guys were throwing. We loved what we did. We believed in the product as superior with no second place and these guys didn't want anyone around who didn't share that passion. The propaganda machine was always running and it fueled our desire to perform.

My tenure as a regional sales manager with Watkins was my first exposure to a belief system. I didn't know it as such at the time, but as I look back on those years relative to what I know today, it is painfully clear that this company and the leaders that comprised its greatness had a belief that permeated through the entire organization like the scent of my grandmother's meat sauce throughout the house on every Sunday that I can remember. The camaraderie among the regional management team was equivalent to a Texas high school football team. The shared passion to win made those years the most memorable in my career. I loved those guys and will value my time with them as critical to understanding the value behind passion and how to lead people using a strong belief system instead of compliance.

When O.T. Neal spoke about salesmanship his spirit became larger than the room. When Steve Hammock presented the marketing campaign and manufacturing evolutions of the product, he was in the zone! And when the regional team was exposed to this passion and belief system, we hit the road like a band of warriors plowing over other hot tub sales reps like a Midwestern wheat field. Compliance and accountability were rarely discussed. I'm not even sure if those words ever came up during the three years I worked there. We delivered huge increases every year because we were inspired, we believed, we knew that consumers were settling for less if they bought any brand other than HotSpring.

I realized through those years that I'm a person who thrives on winning people over. For someone who is virtually inept athletically, this is the game I play and can win over and over again. If I'm going up against another salesperson competing for my business, I know that the experience I provide and the passion I demonstrate with each customer can be the deciding factor in securing his or her business more often than not.

My desire to raise the level of passion within service industries is so strong, that I attempt creating memorable experiences as the customer as well in the hope that it will have some affect on the way other customers are treated. Recently I returned a rental car at Chicago O'Hare airport. Day in and day out, the associates who walk up to a customer returning a car to process the transaction are typically met with indifference by the customer. Business travelers are typically wrapped up in a BlackBerry moment or conversation with their business associates. Families are rushing to make their flight. Most times these types of opportunities to make a memorable experience are passed up because the encounter is perceived as insignificant in the general scheme of things. Yet I see this as a perfect opportunity to create a memorable experience for someone. I firmly believe that each human encounter provides me with an opportunity to demonstrate how creating a memorable experience is effortless relative to its long-term effects.

On this particular day, I was approached by a woman of European descent. As I opened my car door she greeted me and made a wonderful attempt at pronouncing my last name. I smiled and repeated my name back to her accentuating each syllable with Italian verve. "Gap-eet-ta-nel-lee" I said waving my arms like a stereotypical Italian caricature. She spoke Italian to me and asked if I could as well. I replied to her that I only knew enough to show off with my friends at Italian restaurants or get beat up in Brooklyn. She laughed heartedly and told me that I had made her day. By the way, it was only 6 a.m.

So I made her day? Maybe, but that was not my intent. My intent rests in the hope that the memorable experience would carry over to her next few customers and might affect the way those customers feel about Hertz. I have no vested interest in Hertz, but like I said earlier, this is the game I enjoy playing and I truly want to see the level of service delivered in America be elevated. Now, imagine the customer experiences she would deliver if she had a team leader who demonstrated such passion and modeled customer experiences in that way.

With the price and products of every rental car company essentially the same; those types of experiences might enhance the brand itself and be the differentiator needed to reach and maintain market dominance.

Passion is infectious. People respond it to it an outward way. Walk by most people today and they generally have a stoic, almost indifferent look on their face. Make eye contact and snap a smile and in most cases, they'll exchange the favor. When I worked at The Bridal Group, we had a receptionist named Vicki. I will never forget her. I made it a point to engage her in light-hearted banter and pleasantries every time I walk in or even called in. Every time I saw her or spoke with her I'd take a few moments to stop, give her a big smile, and ask an innocuous question about her day. She would instantaneously light up and deliver a warm and cheerful "good morning" that to me had a bit more passion and enthusiasm than the greetings she delivered to those who walked by her as if she was part of the furniture. And I assure you, when she answered an incoming call of one of my customers, friends or relations, the reflection of our 10-second memorable moment earlier that day shined through the way she spoke to them.

You might be saying to yourself that this sounds very much like the story line behind the movie Pay It Forward with Kevin Spacey. Exactly; like I said before, this is not revolutionary. This initial lesson of creating a memorable experience became a common thread with every personal and professional encounter in my life.

So, you should get the idea by now that I firmly believe that each human encounter is an opportunity to create a memorable experience, show your passion and develop significant relationships. Without it, I believe that experiences delivered to customers come off as rote set of techniques or processes that customers are indifferent to. And I've always said that I would rather have someone dislike me than be indifferent to me. Love and hate are emotions; indifference is a void of emotion.

Up to now, passion has been the focal point of this chapter and one could make the argument that passion is an internal mechanism that can't be mandated or created by another person. That may be true. Passion is just the ticket to the dance. But should one need to know how to dance as well, passion will fuel the desire to learn how and learn more.

But, in order for the retail street fighter to get even the most apathetic employee to step up their consideration for serving another person requires an understanding of what fuels passion and ultimately drives a person's behavior and actions—thoughts and beliefs.

The next chapter will explore what it takes for any retailer, whether a single store quilting shop or a national chain of jewelry stores, to reach higher levels of behavioral consistency. Prepare yourself for The CAP Zone.

Enter The CAP Zone

"There is nothing random about making sales."

ArnieCAP

Chapter 3:

Enter The CAP Zone

In this chapter we are going to explore different ways of attempting behavioral consistency (the new term for compliance). One method uses high levels of accountability and making everything a policy under threat of progressive discipline and consequences. Another hopes consistency will occur by treating people nicely and trying to impress upon them the importance of the behavior using influence that is void of disciplinary action. And the final would be a blending of both systems where behavioral change occurs by creating a belief system, employing a disciplined approach to superior customer experiences, monitoring performance to identify gaps in behavior and finally driving the message home with consistent and unrelenting messaging about serving customers.

Here is a simple example of a method driven only by fear of consequence. How often have you been driving down a freeway and noticed you are pushing the speed limit by a good 8 to 12 miles per hour? Not a problem, until you round a bend and see a police officer in the median strip. Your initial reaction (even if you're not speeding) is to lighten the load on your gas pedal—c'mon…you know it's true. So let's be frank, do you creep your car back down to the speed limit because you have a strong belief system regarding the benefits of driving at a safe and legal speed, or is it because you have a sudden anxiety that you might get caught? My guess is the later; primarily because if your beliefs regarding safe driving were engaged and you were aware and committed to satisfying the belief, you wouldn't have been speeding in the first place. In most cases, people believe that the speed limit is there for reckless drivers who are careening and weaving in and out of traffic, but because most don't view themselves as such, there isn't a strong belief about adhering to the posted speed limit.

Here is a simple example of a method driven only by emotional influence with empty threats of consequence and no follow up. In air travel there is a rule that laptops and portable electronic devices have to be powered down during take-off and landing. We're told that it interrupts the navigation systems. Does anyone actual believe that? Not that I can tell. I watched on the morning of Feb. 17, 2009, a grown man sitting in seat 5A of a Delta flight from Atlanta to Memphis (you know who you are) work on his BlackBerry right through take-off. It was comical to watch him pretend to not have it on; flipping it over and hiding it like an 11-year-old hiding his comics in a history book every time the teacher walked by. A grown business man, can you imagine!? The flight attendant made several attempts to impress upon him the importance of powering down the device and used different methods to influence the correct behavior. However, this was done to no avail because the traveler knew that the request had no teeth.

This final example is a method driven by blending emotional influence with a disciplined approach to behavioral changed and backing it up with hard data that results in a self fulfilling prophecy of accountability. A man goes to see his doctor for an annual check up. The man makes attempts to live a healthy life style, but he cheats here and there with fatty food and doesn't exercise as often as he admits too. The doctor informs the man that his weight has increased steadily over the years, but more alarming is that his cholesterol has reached dangerous levels.

The doctor shows the man his charts and numbers and begins to ask him about his eating habits and exercise regimen. The man offers up the truth. The doctor impresses upon the man that in order to live a long and healthy life, he needs to be more disciplined about his nutrition and exercise. The doctor outlines a specific diet and cardio program designed to improve his chances of lowering his cholesterol. The doctor impresses upon the man that he must be aware of times when he is not being disciplined and asks him to commit to the plan. The doctor tells him that ultimately his behavior and disciplined approach is his responsibility, but the numbers will point out that if his cholesterol level doesn't drop within the next six months, it may lead to a more serious course of action. So although the doctor won't be able to monitor every decision or action the man takes, ultimately his behavior will show up on the charts and will determine what happens next.

So now let's talk about this at the store level. For decades, retailers have been trying to get their salespeople to stop saying "Can I help you?" when customers come in the store because they know that the vast majority of shoppers will respond, "No thanks, I'm just looking." At that point the salesperson will drift away and may even blurt a mechanical response of supplying their name and offering assistance should any be required.

In this situation a retailer might attempt to implement a policy, non-negotiable standard, or best practice that customers can't be greeted with such a line under penalty of progressive discipline. Other retailers may attempt to strongly recommend that it not be done, but won't enforce it. In both situations, behavioral consistency will have modest success unless the salesperson has the natural inclination to engage a customer without saying, "Can I help you?"

So what's the solution? Well, have the policy; that's fine. Or try to influence the behavior by talking about it all the time if that's your style. But if behavioral consistency at the highest level is what you are truly looking for, then you must drive the desired behavior through unrelenting messages about your belief regarding how customers are to be greeted. Then hold the salesperson accountable for what they were hired to do, make sales. The truth is this; policies are for operational components of the store. That's it, period! Maintaining performance expectations are for the selling and service side of the business. In other words, if a salesperson is violating policy like chronic tardiness, paperwork issues, inventory process and such, then write 'em up. A retail street fighter can't be caught up in such petty issues. The fight will be an embarrassment if the street fighter is consumed with chasing simple operational policy issues. Conversely, if a salesperson is underperforming relative to baseline productivity metrics, it's a clear sign they are not serving a customer. That's reality. I promise you, I can get a team of salespeople to greet the customer in a way that aligns with my vision for the customer experience without having the threat of severe consequence every time they open their mouth or banging my head against the wall with constant reminding.

Instead of having policy regarding how to behave with a customer, the answer lies in knowing that a superior customer experience has a defined set of disciplines for how to satisfy the belief that customers deserve an experience that is consistent and superior to those of other retailers. Then measure it. If the salesperson cannot sustain performance at a set minimum, they lose the right to serve your customers.

For example:

If you had a shared belief that all customer experiences should be consistent and superior, then in order to satisfy that belief, salespeople would have to be aware of how they were going to engage a customer. The disciplines would suggest:

- Customers should be greeted in a way that engages them and invokes positive conversation.
- Greetings should be warm, welcoming and sincere.

- Salespeople should practice awareness of how a customer is responding to the engagement.

Although these seem ambiguous, they are not meant to be specific behavior that is set in stone as policy. They are meant to be a disciplined approach to serving customers. And when delivered consistently, the belief is satisfied. And if the salesperson is not consistent with these disciplines, it will show up in their performance.

I would never impute a consequence on a salesperson for asking, "Can I help you?" Seriously, is that the kind of pressure you want to put on a 10-year veteran who also happens to be a million dollar writer, and has a great way of engaging the customer with the phrase, "Can I help you?" Trust me, I've tried this; in the long run it doesn't work. If it did, that opening line would be gone by now. Again, if the salesperson is not engaging customers, then it'll show up in their performance. We'll discuss base productivity rates in a later chapter, but in the meantime, let's get into how a retail operator can effectively and methodically get salespeople to behave in a way that serves the customer and company.

To begin with, illustrated below, are the three "zones" a retailer can fall into when attempting to get people to behave with a high degree of behavioral consistency for serving the customer.

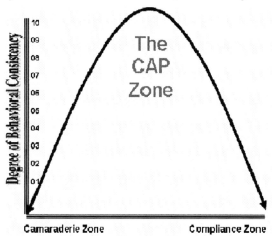

The Camaraderie Zone:

At one end of the spectrum is The Camaraderie Zone, often found in single to three store operations that are category specific merchants (i.e. fitness equipment stores, bike shops, local jewelry stores). I classify these businesses as Professional Owner Operated Retailers (aka POOR). The owners of these stores are very involved and present on the floor. They engage with customers, handle the cash and most of their decisions come from heart and instinct. They make attempts to get the staff to buy-in using motivation, camaraderie and Kumbaya moments. Everyone is treated like family and the operator believes that if the staff likes or respects him, they will do what is expected. I often hear these retailers say, "Can you give me advice on how to write up my mother-in-law?"

Some core attributes of The Camaraderie Zone Retailer:

- Relies heavily on emotional influence as the method for behavioral consistency.

- If accountability and consequences are nothing more than idle threats or flat out non-existent, then the associate will resolve to their own beliefs about how to behave. They'll come to the natural assumption that the desires of the supervisor are really more suggestive than mandated.

- Managers and supervisors quickly grow tired of reminding an associate repetitively about behaviors associated with the customer experience. They consider loyalty and tenure core attributes and so tend to overlook inconsistent or non-compliant behavior unless it puts the store at risk. These retailers feel there is too much anxiety over having to find a replacement as a good enough reason not to force the issue and don't want to be perceived by the staff as heavy-handed.

Some common phrases of The Camaraderie Zone Retailer:

- If I treat them well, they'll do it.

- Can we all just get along?
- I know he can't sell, but he's such a loyal employee.
- She's been here forever; she's like family.

The Camaraderie Zone Retailer can be successful in this model as long as they don't have plans to grow past their ability to touch every particle that moves through the company. Employees provide them some relief to take a day off or the once per decade vacation.

As illustrated in the chart above, a store that uses a camaraderie model at the extreme end is hoping the staff will behave properly out of respect for the family and a sense of obligation. The Camaraderie Zone Retailer can do quite well at the polar end of the scale as long as they don't have any plans to expand much. As this retailer grows, their ability to get behavioral consistency diminishes as their ability to be omnipresent wanes. The spirit of the family becomes diluted as the organization grows. As the Camaraderie Zone Retailer expands, they often become frustrated if they begin to experience a lack of behavioral consistency. Oftentimes the desperate retailer responds by swinging the pendulum the other direction into the Compliance Zone.

The Compliance Zone:

At the other end of the spectrum is The Compliance Zone, most commonly found in multi-unit brands. I classify these retailers as Business Executives And Strategic Thinkers (aka B.E.A.S.T.). These retailers attempt conformity via non-negotiable rules and standards and time restrictive performance accountability. This model leaves little room for deviation from the plan. This model requires a human resource department that is in high gear every time an employee is accused of burping in the wrong direction.

The Compliance Zone Retailer has a forest of reports that the DM uses to find a ray of light for the conference call. Turnover is a fact of life.

Some core attributes of The Compliance Zone Retailer:

- Relies on accountability messages as the method for behavioral consistency.

- Is often more consumed with operational compliance. Low revenue performance is blamed on traffic or assortment.

- If a customer service standard is in place, but the salesperson thinks his way is better, he will do what he believes is right because he knows he will most likely get away with it or might even be successful with it at times. And even if the associate is trained with the "correct" way and can prove it in role-playing, he will try to get away with it any chance he gets if he doesn't believe the alternative method is any better than his.

- Store managers in this system resent having to play cop to procedures that aren't a pebble in the shoe of loss prevention and steer away from imputing consequences because in many cases he has developed friendships with the staff and doesn't want the image of being a hard-ass. Also, the payroll strapped and report laden store manager can't get out enough to recruit and ends up hiring warm bodies when the pain of being understaffed is too great to bear. Often the store manager tries to run his own store with a camaraderie model inside a company that expects compliance.

Some common phrases of The Compliance Zone Retailer:

- This is not negotiable.

- When I want your opinion, I'll give it to you.

- If this happens again, I'll have to write you up.

- It's my way or the highway.

The Compliance Zone Retailer can be successful with the model as long as the retailer has an ongoing recruiting campaign and the store organization has a great support mechanism with HRD. A communications department is needed that can ensure all documentation is clear, specific, and has follow up mechanisms in place. Consistency with progressive discipline is a must. The field team leaders tend to be consumed with operational integrity because it's easy to validate and fix. It's also what they are most accountable for.

An operation that employs a strict accountability model, operating with extremely detailed standards for performance and behavioral compliance, is banking on the idea that employees will comply if the consequences are severe enough. They create specific policy and procedure documents, plan-o-grams and other communication vehicles that clearly spell out how things must be done. The compliance model works well as long as the message that negotiation of the standards carries severe consequences and is permeating down the ranks into the stores. Success relies heavily on store managers being diligent with documenting non-compliance and following up with consequences.

Again, I'd like to point out that both of these models can work just fine provided the liabilities can be rationalized. Many retailers do just fine with camaraderie and have no desire to grow the number of stores they have. Many use compliance and know how to recruit people who share that style and so they deal with the turn over and stick with the plan.

However, the retail street fighter must be aware that there is a kryptonite factor for both zones; a character trait in most people that will prevent these retailers from reaching higher levels of behavioral consistency. The kryptonite of both the Compliance and Camaraderie Zones is called "self-intendedness".

Self-intendedness is a condition that exists in every human. It basically means that every person is ultimately behaving in a way to satisfy their personal wants, needs and desires. Self-intendedness means, "I do what I believe is right for me."

Self-Intended people can work in a high compliance model if the anxiety of losing their job is compelling enough. It can also work in the high camaraderie model because reciprocation of loyalty is important to them. However, this typically achieves only minimum levels of execution with desired behaviors, especially relative to the customer experience. This is because the associate knows its being done for external reasons, not to satisfy an internal belief system.

To put this in to simple terms:
The external driver: "I'll do this because it's required."
The internal driver: "I'll do this because I understand."

The CAP Zone:

So if the retailer truly wants to reach higher levels of behavioral consistency, he/she must enter "The CAP Zone," which has an objective of getting the associate to develop a connection with the internal driver—their belief system; which is driving their thoughts and behavior.

CAP is an acronym for Customer Advocate Programs and is the basis for this book. The essence of customer advocacy is that the customer service model is built on a foundation of attributes that works with self-intendedness as opposed to attempting behavioral consistency in spite of it. The great thing about the CAP Zone is that both single store operators and multi-unit chains can benefit from using it, because it is essentially a blending of both models.

Some core attributes of The CAP Zone

• Uses customer feedback to define the customer experience.

- Relies heavily on addressing the belief system, not attacking behavior as the method for achieving higher levels of behavioral consistency.

- Wanting to serve customers is the ticket to the dance. Varying degrees of apathy towards serving and selling is unacceptable (their belief system is too strong).

- Behavioral compliance is reserved for operational policy violations. Performance trends are used to identify gaps in the customer experience and become the basis for skill development or corrective action.

- Managers enlist coaching skills designed to cause associates to self-discover the behaviors required to improve performance.

- Consistent performance "below the line" becomes the true objective method for disciplinary measures.

Once higher levels of service becomes a core belief, is apparent culturally in the business model and chasing operational compliance is not tolerated, then supervisors are freed up to tap into the innate desire and pre-existing skills the associates have to serve others.

The CAP Zone's formula for success is:
- Identify your customers' expectations for service.
- Define the belief system for your customer experience.
- Create the disciplines that support the beliefs.
- Develop an awareness to gauge progress and expose service experience erosion.
- Be relentlessly committed to the cause.

What keeps a retailer out of The CAP Zone?

Through the years, there have been a couple of prevailing conditions that have kept retailers from reaching higher levels of behavioral consistency. The sum of it all is that the expectation to comply is placed within the ranks of the front line, training becomes the vehicle to "fix" everything, and the effort is viewed as a program that is expected to sustain itself.

This has failure written all over it. The key to the gateway of behavioral consistency; the only way to get into the CAP Zone is by adhering to these 3 basic principles:

1. Have a defined and repetitive message from the most senior person in the organization about how customers are to be served.

2. The decision makers must ensure that every initiative aligns with the company's beliefs and how it will affect the customer experience.

3. The field organization cannot allow the small, tactile pieces of running an operation overshadow the larger, more "spiritual" dynamics of serving customers.

Its now time to dig into each component of The CAP Zone and provide detail for gaining knowledge about what customers expect when they enter your store and how to create your own CAP Zone model. The next chapter will address how to define a belief system and the steps necessary to create one within your organization. Once that is defined, we will then go through the moves needed to win the street fight so your business can grow and thrive.

You Gotta Believe

"The brand defines the beliefs, beliefs drive behavior, behavior elevates the brand."

ArnieCAP

Retail Street Fight

Chapter 4:

You Gotta Believe

At this point we're going to dig a little deeper into the elements of The CAP Zone. However, it must be noted that in order to get a better understanding of how to develop a belief system and the underlying disciplines and accountability benchmarks, there must be a working knowledge of exactly what customers are saying about your store and about your shopping experience. The only way you can really develop an experience that exceeds your customers' expectations is by getting feedback from your customers about the experience they want. So if you're not using customer feedback tools like NPS and Mystery Shop Reports, then you're really missing the boat. You're basing all of your experience models on hearsay or what you believe is important. Once customer expectations are known, a company can build a set of Core Beliefs that define how to exceed those expectations.

So, what is Belief System? Everyone has a core set of values that guide their decisions and behaviors every day. This is what I refer to as a belief system. Belief systems are typically ignited and driven by a central figure or iconic person who defines the beliefs and delivers the message consistently, repetitively and with conviction. It can grow provided it is seeded and nurtured by passionate people who align themselves with the leader's powerful vision and message. The belief system guides our thoughts and actions and, more importantly, how we interact with others. The stronger the belief system in an individual, the more consistently they behave—even when the central figure is not present.

Followers or disciples of a defined belief system see this person as a well of inspiration. They are moved by the unbending relentlessness to realize the vision that underlies the beliefs. This icon need not be the purveyor of a new truth, nor does he or she need to be the original source of an existing vision. I have also found that the person does not require some over-the-top evangelical delivery style. In fact, in my case, some of the people who molded my belief system are not type-A personalities. They are not flashy, nor require the center of attention. Their power and largeness of being comes from the internal passion they have to serve people and bring the vision to reality. The organization is inspired by the consistency of the message and the drive to realize the vision. They refer to the belief system as the foundation for every decision and behavior required by the team right down to the front line organization. The belief system then permeates the organization so each layer represents the vision with similar passion, conviction, consistency and repetitiveness.

Recovering addicts are a perfect example of how a belief system defines behavior. Let me start by making a direct statement that I hope won't offend, it just happens to be true. Smoking, over-eating and alcohol and substance abuse is detrimental to the health and well being of one's body. That is an indisputable fact. Yet we find people today, with all the facts and consequences known still engaging in this kind of behavior. Why? Haven't the steps for recovery been defined? There certainly are plenty of statistics that validate the findings, and the consequences are known. So what keeps this behavior engaged? If the person's desire to quit is driven by compliance and fear, the change is destined to fail. If the person's core belief is that the addictive behavior is "not a problem," then that will perpetuate the addictive behavior. Compliance and fear is no match for a belief system, even if the belief system is counter productive to the body's desire to thrive.

Step in weight loss clinics, Alcoholics Anonymous, and smoking secession hypnotherapies. These organizations all have steps, disciplines and standards for changing unwanted behavior. So why do some clients stay with the program and others abandon it? The ones achieving success align with an organization or support system that is successful at shifting or evolving the belief system as opposed to attacking the behavior. Success is heavily reliant on getting to the core of a person's beliefs about "self" and aligning it with the body's need to survive and thrive. By having a vision of what is possible, developing a belief system that supports growth, defining the steps to getting there, and having an individual or support team relentlessly communicate those dynamics to the individual in a supporting, and firm way, a new belief system can emerge and behavioral change is manifested and is sustained.

Certainly there are plenty of psychological implications here regarding why someone engages in self-destruction, and I'm not going to pretend for a second that I have a working knowledge of it. But, regardless of background, education and upbringing, there are proven cases of individuals from all walks of life who have changed counter-productive behavior as a result of a new or evolved belief system. These people have stepped beyond compliance and fear and entered the world of engaging in behaviors that promote health and wellbeing because they believe. Fortunately, all we are trying to do is deliver great customer experiences. This isn't nearly as compelling as quitting smoking, but the concept is the same. I assure you if we can get diehard smokers and over-eaters to change they way they think about themselves, and have them behaving in a way that promotes health, then we can get store associates to deliver superior experiences in a way that promotes growth.

Beliefs and the Customer Experience

In order to develop and define a company's beliefs regarding the customer experience, one must first determine how a customer wants to experience the store. From self-serve to assisted serve to full serve, the expectations are likely to be different, or possibly more demanding as the product assortment requires more assistance.

How much do you know about your customer and their expectations of your establishment? Are you dialed into what they really want from your service model once the initial motivator of product has been satisfied? As merchants (especially category specialists) there may be the assumption that the products being carried are products customers want. So if you have it, and they want it, then they'll buy it, right? Not so fast. If you're the only one in town that carries that product and there are no catalogues or virtual storefronts that compete against you with that specific product line, then sure, you would be absolutely correct. Those of you who work for The American Girl Doll Store, stand up and cheer; this describes you perfectly. And by the way, have you been into an American Girl Doll Store? They're packed, all the time, and have an incredible experience in spite of it. The rest of you…read on.

The key to differentiation in an industry of "sameness" is the experience a customer has with an individual working in your store. In terms of price and efficiency, the Internet, mass merchants and catalogues will always make it very easy for the customer to get what they want. If we can take pause for a moment and actually look at a single customer standing in a brick and mortar store, the scenario begs asking the question "why?" What possible reason could there be for a consumer to be standing in a retail store anymore? What are they hoping will happen here that they feel might be the better alternative to shopping price and efficiency?

I recently contracted to have a patio put in my backyard. Thus I need patio furniture, and a new grill, and whatever else catches my eye. So this past memorial weekend, the Capitanelli family hit a well-known specialty backyard retailer just outside the Mall of Georgia, a well-known retail hotspot. This retailer carries not only patio furniture, but spas, grills, fire pits, accessories and everything else I would want.

Long story short—not even a hello from the two people standing behind the counter. We, five in total, were never acknowledged. We walked the floor, touched everything, used the bathroom, sat on products, and 15 minutes later, we walked out. We were thanked by the young man who was washing windows outside the store for visiting. Visiting? Are you kidding me? We reeked of ideal customer. And it was Memorial Day weekend! Retail street fight—lost.

Allow me to privy you to the conversation these associates had with their boss later that day.

Boss: "How'd you do today; any business?"
Associate: "Not really. It was slow. Ya know the economy is really hurtin' us around here. Blah, blah, blah."

Now, unless the company employs a traffic counter (which everyone should have—get on with it already!) then there is no way to refute that associate's reply.

Any retailer who buys into the idea that customers should be served in their store is making a huge mistake if they don't take a portion of their marketing dollars and get some feedback from their customers about what their service expectations are. Three of the most fundamental rules of retailing:

1. Know how many people are coming into your store.

2. Find out how it went.

3. Ask if they would come back and refer others.

It is extremely important that the experiences we create be consistent with what we know are the primary expectations of shoppers who are now in the market for the products you sell. This experience must also be consistent from customer to customer and in every store, and the experience must actually exceed the customer's expectations.

So what do we know about what a customer wants? Obviously I can't speak to the specifics for your industry and the type of people who shop your store, but globally speaking here's the list. And by the way, if these seem obvious to you, then it's only because the list is logical. Ask your staff to compile a list from scratch, see if it matches this one. More importantly, pit their answers and this against the realities of your store, then tell me how obvious this list seems.

- Value – Everything seems expensive until value has been established. But value is more about satisfying a personal need than it is about saving money. To the customer, value is established through a product attribute that connects to a personal want, the environment itself, and the experience delivered by the salesperson. As those elements impact the customer, the price is rationalized.

- Service Readiness – Customers deserve a store that is prepared to serve them. With the ease of shopping on the Internet and in catalogues, our preparedness to serve is not a luxury, it's a necessity. It is one of the only differentiators specialty retailers have today. They chose to shop in the brick and mortar environment for a reason. If the store is not customer ready, then why bother going to it.

- Product Knowledge – Customers want to be properly educated on the products they show interest in. Not necessarily in terms of what it is or what it has, but how product features translate into personal benefits to the customer. Having the largest or best selection of merchandise available is useless if associates aren't equipped to communicate properly to the customer. This requires store associates having tools that can assist in product knowledge and can better translate product attributes into "personal buying motivators".

- Service Attentiveness – The level of service provided customers should not parallel the price position of the assortment. In other words, low price does not dictate low service. If the same person can work in either an express motel or a high-end luxury resort, then the only difference in service are the amenities each respective facility offers. But that should not be a reflection of how attentive, friendly and accommodating the employee should be to the customer.

- Listening Skills – Unless born with a physiological impairment, everyone can hear. It essentially never turns off. But there is a real distinction between hearing and listening. Our ears are in a constant state of picking up all the sounds and noises, chirping and barking and, of course, dialogues and conversations occurring around us every day. However, this does not mean that we are actively listening to something specific that we purposely dial into. Hearing is a sense, listening is a skill. Many believe they are good listeners mostly because hearing comes so natural. But without the intent to listen actively, the natural process of hearing is not sufficient enough to fully understand what customers are telling us. Everyone wants to be heard. Salespeople and CSRs and anyone who engages a customer need to be attentive and understanding of customer needs. This means we need to not only "hear" what is being said, but also to remember. This places a great deal of emphasis on how well detailed information is documented for follow up, prospecting and customer be-back visits. Listening is the quintessential skill for all professionals.

- Consistency – It has been said that no two customers are alike, however, that doesn't mean that there shouldn't be a similarity in the way all customers experience the store. Consistency in key components of the customer experience is critical to how a customer perceives the experience.

Now that we have a better understanding of what our customers want and expect, we need to define our beliefs for how we will fulfill these expectations. A Belief System is more than a mission statement about a company. It's a working, cultural doctrine about how associates should serve customers. Your expectation should be that each and every store employee, including CSRs, has an understanding that the beliefs and disciplines about service define how customers experience the store, which ultimately affects the decision to purchase as well as how much.

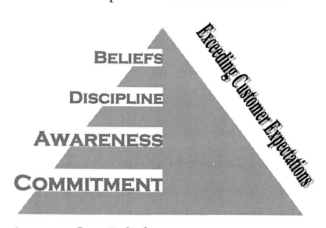

Creating your Core Beliefs

Think about what you strongly believe in. Think about how those beliefs and values drive you to make certain decisions, engage specific behaviors and participate in gratifying activities. In the book Being There—Sometimes Good Intentions are Simply Not Enough, authors Dr. Derek Smyth and Robert Jones point out that on the basis of cognitive therapy the way a person thinks determines how that person will feel and behave. The way we think about a process, an event, a person or a situation forms the feelings we have about that process, event, person or situation. For example, imagine you are on a very crowded bus or train after a long, arduous day at the office. You are holding onto a strap to keep your balance, but there are people all around you pressing against you. It's hot, smelly, and crowded. Suddenly you are jabbed in your side by someone's elbow. It really hurts. "What the…" you think as you swing around to confront the offender.

Most people would feel quite annoyed at being jabbed like that in such a situation (most likely stemming from the initial feeling of disrespect or unimportance). Chances are the initial thought would manifest a feeling of anger and the resulting behavior might be that you would clench your hand, or turn to the person and "tell them off" or even just mumble under your breath, "Some people are so rude." These feelings and behaviors all were triggered by the belief that someone was inconsiderate to you.

So you turn to the person, jaw clenched, ready to say or do something but as you turn you noticed that the person who jabbed you was blind. It is likely the initial feeling of anger subsides as you realize the blind person jabbed you unintentionally. The feeling of anger may not only subside but may actually evolve into feelings of sympathy and concern. Instead of telling him off, you ask, "Are you ok?" This new behavior is caused by a new thought or belief about the situation.

What this suggests is that the behavioral reaction comes from how we think or the perception of what occurred. As a result, these theorists believe that if we change the way we think about things, we can change the way we feel about it. That change manifests in behavioral changes as well.

So, relative to behavior associated with the customer experience is that if a person's thoughts, perceptions and beliefs can be addressed in a way that creates a new thought, perception and belief, then the resulting behavior is driven by an internal mechanism (the associate's beliefs) as opposed to an external mechanism (compliance or motivation).

Over the years, I helped quite a few retailers develop their core beliefs. Again, this is not a mission statement or corporate culture; these are a way of thinking, a way of life. Below are core beliefs that are a blending of the ones I've helped develop. They are the foundation for the customer experience and the spirit behind the disciplines that define it.

CAP Beliefs

 Every customer experience is consistent and exceeds the customer's expectations—serve the underserved.

 Communication is critical to brand loyalty.

 Represent the company with core values of responsibility and commitment.

If you recall from the previous chapter was the example of attempting to remove "Can I help you?" from the customer experience using compliance or camaraderie. Before that initiative can even be broached, the associate would have to have a full understanding of what the true objective is when engaging a customer and would have to employ behaviors that satisfy the objective.

So are the words "Can I help you?" so offensive to people that it should be permanently banned from the sales floor or is it the spirit of the delivery and the behaviors/attitudes the associate enlists when saying it that prevents the customer from wanting to engage?

I know this for sure; I have used very creative unique and special opening lines on customers and still heard "No thanks, I'm just looking," as a response. I have also been at a loss for words when encountering a customer and inquired in a most sincere way "Is there anything I can help you with?" and ended up with my new BFF.

My belief that a customer should experience me in a way that extends a high desire to help them with their purchases colors my greeting with sincerity, curiosity and desire. My goal is to engage them and I will do that with a greeting that is appropriate for the moment and based on how I assess their openness to be engaged.

I prefer to avoid saying "Can I help you?" because I think it's hacked. So when attempting to engage customers, I assess their style and personality the best I can on first impression, gauge the level of "outgoingness" I think will cause them to engage, and approach them in a way that puts them at ease. The words and tone I use lets the customer know that the service model is customer centric. Sometimes I can fly with something unique and inspired by the moment. Sometimes I sense that I need to soft approach and will nod the customer's way saying something light like, "So are ya having fun today?" And then there are the times I'm stuck and all I have is the standard. But no matter what I say or do to engage the customer, this is for sure; it is said with honest sincerity, curiosity, and a desire to serve. If the customer is not ready to be engaged, the goal would be to remain watchful while she is assimilating to the store.

And when you really have a store that understands the customer experience at the highest level, the salesperson may decide that another salesperson is better suited to serve the customer. That topic will be approached in Chapter 7.

Once a belief system has been created, the retail street fighter can begin to take a disciplined approach to winning the fight of out-serving the opponent.

They are armed with very cool weapons. They have technology, process efficiency, huge marketing budgets, better margins, ease of shopping, etc. You have the experience. Somewhat of a David vs. Goliath story line, but we know how that turned out. The retail street fighter can't take their only weapon and use it haphazardly or randomly. There has to be a disciplined approach, especially if the behaviors required to exceed customer expectations are not consistent or natural in your service model.

The next chapter will go into great detail about how I came to realize that a disciplined approach to the experience can drive success, regardless of your business model.

The Dreaded Pretzel Hold

"Training creates compliance—learning creates behavior. Long-term, evolutionary changes to behavior can only come by creating a disciplined learning environment. As the learning environment influences the belief system, the 'correct' behaviors will follow."

ArnieCAP

Chapter 5:

The Dreaded Pretzel Hold

For the first eight years following high school, I relied on retail sales jobs as a way to earn a living without needing a formal education. I quickly learned that commission was my best option because if I needed more money, I would just sell more stuff or higher ticket items. I sold clothes, shoes, vacuum cleaners and home furnishings. Through each of those sales jobs, I had no real sense of why I was good at selling other than I simply believed that passion and personality were the ticket. I realize now that I had no right to declare myself good at selling unless I had a method for measuring my performance and identifying the disciplines required to close more sales.

Regardless, I knew not every presentation ended in a sale and I was plagued with a burning question. Why would someone who experienced virtually the same sales presentation for the same product as a customer who bought, choose not to buy from me? And make no mistake; I did view this as a choice—a conscious decision by the customer to not buy from me.

In 1987 when Bill Hanoucek recruited me to his hot tub store, I was still looking for the answer to this question. During my first week on the job, Bill sat me down in front of a TV and a VHS machine. He instructed me to take a few days to review this eight-tape series of The 7 Steps of Successful Retail Selling by retail training guru Harry J. Friedman. "Learn how to sell?" I thought. I can't afford to be off the floor to watch tapes about something I already do instinctively. How wrong I was.

Unless converting at 100 percent, each lost sale is an opportunity to reflect on why a customer chose not to buy. But if you don't know what you are doing in terms of steps and techniques, then you don't know what to fix. Just try to fix your golf swing without knowing the fundamentals of the swing plane and the physics of ball contact. Even if you could manage to hit two out of every five shots perfectly without a lesson, you'll never know how to fix the three out of five you shanked. That could mean the difference between a double-bogie and a par. On the sales floor, it's called conversion rate—meaning six out of 10 customers are choosing to buy from someone else. The salesperson will say to management; "If you want me to sell more people, send me more customers (meaning increase traffic through higher marketing costs)". The insightful Mr. Friedman would reply, "Why don't you just learn how to sell more of the people you are already getting?"

Harry Friedman's sales training program changed the way I looked at selling forever. Selling and serving customers was no longer an improvisational, free-flowing exchange of words peppered with passion, wit and an underlying need to keep my '74 240Z away from the repo-man. Success on the sales floor was a carefully choreographed series of steps that guided a customer to a decision to purchase. Now don't get me wrong, I am not a proponent of canned, scripted dialogue used to manipulate a customer into buying. But I do believe that accomplished salespeople who use passion as the primary ingredient to delivering super experiences can know where a sales presentation is going and how well they are doing by following a logical sequence of objectives meant to build a relationship and establish value.

Take for example an accomplished guitarist who can run his fingers up and down the frets in a seemingly effortless way—notes being selected so randomly that no two solos are exactly the same. To the layman, these improvisational riffs seem like free-flowing genius. But the reality is that these musicians have spent years studying and practicing theory and technique. The random notes they are playing actually follow a well-defined chord structure and timing pattern. And anyone who thinks they can achieve that level of musicianship without knowing theory, timing and without practicing is sadly mistaken.

By the way, this analogy works for the likes of Tiger Woods, Michael Jordan and Jerry Rice, to name a few. Their genius on their given field of play is only possible through years of understanding and drilling the fundamentals of their athletic prowess. Their experience with the fundamentals got them to the game, their passion and drive makes them great.

Certainly selling is less glamorous than music and sports—but the theory is the same. And what I learned watching these tapes is that every successful sale had some common thread components to them. Each component was comprised of an objective and Harry's techniques to achieve the objective.

Initially, I immersed myself in the literal techniques of the program. I tried desperately to actualize each technique exactly as presented in the videos. Many of the techniques were awkward, some never became natural, and some customers took control of the sale and I couldn't get them to follow the steps. But I was bound and determined to own these techniques; so much so that I eventually went to work for The Friedman Group so I could train others on this program.

I traveled the globe speaking proudly and convincingly that if a retailer wasn't using this method, they were not maximizing the potential of the store. This was the way to sell in retail, no question about it. As mentioned earlier, I went as far as to insist that salespeople execute selling behaviors as if standard operating procedure; going as far as to say that if they didn't "sell this way" they could lose their jobs. However, as training programs ended with a particular company, and I moved onto another retailer in another part of the world, I experienced a lingering anxiety that the program could have a shelf life. And as mentioned previously in the camera story at the beginning of the book, this more often than not was true.

I left The Friedman Group in late 1994 and went to work for one of the most famous musical instrument stores in the world, Manny's Music on 48th street in Manhattan. My goal was to prove once and for all that a retail business model built on specific behaviors and techniques coupled with high levels of performance accountability could be sustained. I was bound to validate that everything I had been training other companies to do was viable at the hands of a highly capable implementer of this program. But when I hit the floor with the program, the resistance to compliance and accountability was palpable. Musical instrument stores are the pinnacle for enthusiast retailing. This store had 30+ salespeople, most of whom were struggling musicians selling instruments to make rent and pay for studio time. Don't get me wrong, these guys could sell. They were straight commission and most were doing quite well. But they were dead set against being immersed into a retail model that invalidated their free-spiritedness and personal style.

The more I pushed, the harder they pushed back. These guys were not going to have it. I tried dozens of ways to get buy-in and compliance. I tried writing tickets, making under-performers attend Saturday morning sales meetings, and I fired anyone who even hinted at unwillingness. I wrote newsletters, ran contests, put up charts with gold stars to highlight top performance. But at the end of the day (3 years to be exact), I was still busting people for saying "Can I help you?" Can you imagine trying to change a 50 year old culture by talking about such a trivial element of the customer experience?

I left Manny's in 1998 having been recruited by David's Bridal. At that point I wasn't convinced that the program it-self was missing something. Surely the problem was the guys at Manny's. So when I began my career at David's Bridal, I knew that if I were driving the training platform in a more typical specialty retail model, I would certainly get compliance. By my six month in that role, the field organization was growing frustrated. The idea that I would attempt tight-rope behavioral compliance was not what they wanted in a training program.

Out of shear desperation, I realized something had to change. I felt like I was trying to drop an oval peg in a round hole. It looked like it would drop right in, but it wasn't a fit.

Thus came the knowledge that behavioral consistency was reliant on first creating a strong belief system. This concept was presented to me that year under the tutelage and mentorship of Robert Huth, president of David's Bridal. During my rookie year there, I developed a deeper understanding that salespeople respond and react better to their own beliefs as opposed to heavy-handed compliance. I came to understand that there was a great need to appreciate how people could naturally satisfy the objective of the customer experience without having them feel like they were bound to a rail of selling behavior with little to no room for disparity.

Mr. Huth sat with me one day and gave me some of the greatest insights to creating behavioral change I had ever heard. He told me that I was focusing too much on process and protocol. And the more I tried to impose my will on the ranks of the store, the more they would resent it and push back. He pushed me to simplify the customer experience in a way that salespeople would understand because it touched them internally and wouldn't be difficult for them to execute. He told me we hired good people who wanted to be successful, make money and get satisfaction out of their job and from the company that provided it.

In time I realized that it was the objective of selling that was more important than the technique itself. If it is agreed that no two customer interactions are exactly the same, then it stands to reason that the common thread with every customer experience is the satisfaction of an objective, not the execution of a technique. So once I began to understand what I was actually trying to accomplish, then my own beliefs and disciplines created a behavioral model that could easily be delivered and replicated on the sales floor.

Instead of making sure salespeople were walking toward the customer exactly the right way or phrasing questions properly, we developed a belief system about what was important to customers when shopping in a retail store. I came to learn that beginning with a great relationship is essential to building lasting ones. I learned that trust was born from curiosity and from the act of discovering what was driving a customer's desires. I saw that value was personal, not manufactured. And most importantly, empathy was critical to getting customers to reveal themselves, so I knew how to alleviate any apprehension they had to buying. Knowing these truths further fueled my passion and they answered that question that had plagued me for years. As my deeper understanding of the objectives of serving customers became clear, mandating techniques were no longer the objective. I ultimately learned that I could engage a customer, build an ample ticket and develop a long-term relationship with them without following rigid rules and demanding specific techniques. The techniques were necessary; after all, no one is born with selling technique. But they weren't compulsory. We had to be disciplined in the way we served and the metrics revealed where the experience was eroding and more specifically the salespeople most responsible for the erosion.

Rather than believe people were non-compliant with process, we worked to un-complicate the process to make it easier for them to succeed. Whenever behavioral deviation was occurring we first questioned whether it was a result of poorly aligned beliefs as opposed to a hidden need to be subversive and undermine the company's goals. If you start with the premise that we don't hire "bad" people, then it's not hard to conclude that sometimes we make it too easy for good people to behave badly.

So rather than write tickets for every moving violation, we did the following:

- We defined our beliefs.

- We identified specific behaviors that we knew supported the belief.

- We bombarded the staff with propaganda and tracked performance to identify gaps in behavior to raise their awareness.

- We were nauseatingly repetitive with this system.

- If a gap in performance appeared, we addressed the beliefs of the salesperson, which in turn caused her to examine the behaviors she needed to be more disciplined with.

So even though the disciplines were positioned as behaviors every customer should experience, the evidence of service erosion was revealed in the metrics we associated with the behavior. For example:

A salesperson at David's Bridal was required to place a headpiece on a bride when she began to indicate that she had a gown on that she liked. Although we had identified this behavior as a "vow" (the term we used for behavioral standard) to the customer experience, it was the satisfaction of the belief that every bride deserved a superior experience that was the objective.

So if a salesperson had a low percentage of headpieces for gown unit sales, we embarked on a mission to ensure she fully understood our beliefs about consistency in the experience and provided the training necessary to show the headpiece. If the stat didn't improve it was an indication that the training and coaching didn't change the behavior. It was at that point we began corrective action. In other words, if the stat stayed flat, it suggested the behavior was compromised. In cases where the stat didn't improve, it was more likely a result of misaligned beliefs about adding on than the ability to do it. So rather than pursue it as a violation of a non-negotiable standard of selling behavior, we hit the associate hard with messaging about our beliefs and how to serve. If performance didn't change, it was decided the associate was either not capable of the skills necessary to serve the customer or their own belief system was counter to the company's beliefs. Either way, if addressing the associate's belief system to discover why she wasn't offering headpieces to every bride didn't fix the under-performing statistic, then further consequences, which may have included termination, would occur because of performance accountability.

Sometimes an associate has a counter-belief; meaning that his/her core belief about the customer experience is contrary to that of the company. When that happens, one can almost guarantee that behavioral consistency will be at a very low level. In one case in an AfterHours Formalwear store, we had a discipline in place about greeting customers when they first entered a store. Research suggested that men shopping for formalwear didn't want to spend a lot of time looking around; especially if they were only there to pay and be fitted as the groomsman in their buddy's wedding.

One day on a store visit, we noticed an employee taking his time to greet a customer. We made attempts to impress upon the employee that we had a Belief that customers expected attentive service based on customer feedback. This made it necessary to greet customers promptly to satisfy that Belief. We reviewed the beliefs and identified metrics that revealed gaps in performance. We scrimmaged with him and validated that he knew how to greet. Yet each time we visited or mystery shopped his store, the behavior was not consistent. So what was the problem? Upon digging into his beliefs about how customers wanted to be treated, he revealed to us that he firmly believed that his customers would prefer to meander around a store for a while before being greeted. In spite of the research, in spite of the realization that we had an 800-sq. ft. store with 20 or so black tuxedos on display for rent, in spite of the fact that groomsmen in particular weren't there to select, just to be fitted and pay, he couldn't get past his core beliefs. Not a lot you can do with a guy with such a strong counter-belief system.

When an existing belief system cannot be changed or modified and the resulting behavioral inconsistency is showing up in performance, the supervisor has no other option than to discuss promoting the associate to customer.

In my travels, I always run into a David's Bridal customer in a speech or seminar I'm delivering. In the middle of the seminar, without any previous relationship or knowledge of the bride, I describe within painful detail exactly what happened when she visited the store. From the greeting, to the acquisition of event information, the selection of gowns, the dressing room experience, the add-on, appointments for alterations and bridesmaid dresses, etc, etc, I relive the experience with her as if I was right there the day she was shopping. Please understand that she is one of thousands and thousands of brides that shopped in one specific David's Bridal in the chain of nearly 200 stores. And it doesn't matter whether she bought or not, nearly every time I do this, the woman confirms the experience I described.

The look on the faces of those in the speech or seminar when I ask them, "If you ran into one of your customers today, could you describe their experience to such detail?" reveals the answer. With all those brides coming in and out of a David's Bridal every week you can imagine how incredibly difficult it would be to hold a salesperson compliant to a specific moment in the customer experience.

Before I go any further, some of you maybe thinking, "Wait, isn't David's Bridal one of those big box category killers I'm trying to compete against?" Well kind of. They have the marketing budget, the value oriented assortment, and process guys creating efficiency, but Mr. Huth and his senior team at David's Bridal never let that be a reason to not serve. The model didn't dictate service. In fact, many systemic improvements were shelved in my 10 years at David's Bridal because the improvement didn't support the salesperson's ability to provide the experience.

In an edition of the NRF publication Stores, I read a brief article called "Bringing It All Together," which discussed how retailers needed to ensure that all their IT solutions, supply chain improvements and backroom processes are being designed with the customer experience in mind. This is great, and on many levels, one would think this should be a given. However, the fact is that many companies I have both worked and provided consulting for literally forgot about the person who delivers the customer experience when developing their systems and operational process solutions.

This is a frightening thought, but it is very true in many cases. All one needs to do on any random weekend is to observe the frustrations that occur regularly in many retailers across the country. I'm not talking about frustrated customers; it's frustrated associates who are convinced that the people responsible for developing solutions haven't spent a day in a store helping customers on a busy Saturday.

But even as significant improvements in process efficiencies have been realized, where many miss the target is forgetting that it's the sales associate who has to deliver the desired experience. So instead of asking, "How do we create a better customer experience?" the real question should be "How do we help our associates better serve our customers?"

Retail street fighters must begin to understand that it's the passion and desire of the sales associate to serve that makes for an exceptional customer experience, not IT solutions and supply chain improvements. Don't get me wrong, IT solutions and supply chain improvements have to occur to stay current and competitive. But if the solution or improvement doesn't include the associate's ability to deliver the experience with relative ease, then the associate's belief that the company has no clue as to what it takes to serve a customer will overshadow the solution. That belief will manifest itself in behaviors steeped in frustration, embarrassment, lack of passion and a quest to figure out how to work around the process.

And let's be frank, the customer has no real connectivity to the people working behind the scenes of these initiatives. It is well known that at nearly every point of sale transaction occurring daily in malls across the country, not a single customer asked for the name of the CIO so she could call and congratulate him for delivering a great customer experience. However, I have been the recipient of many customer service phone calls, letters and e-mails (both good and bad) and I will tell you with the highest degree of confidence that an overwhelming majority of them named store associates as the person responsible for disappointment or satisfaction. In some cases, the complaints clearly pointed to supply chain and delivery failures, but it was still the associate who the consumer held responsible for the experience.

The experience drives the purchase. The process supports the experience. This brings us to defining the disciplines that underlie the beliefs.

When I consult with a company, I take into consideration whether or not the company has a pre-existing selling system or training program they are using to teach technique or develop skills. If so, I want to make sure that I can blend it into the experience being developed for them. I break down the entire customer experience into four distinct moments; so if the retailer has specific closing tools, collateral materials, certain scripts they use to describe a product or service, I look to weave them into to the learning platform being created. Don't get me wrong, there are techniques in my program. Selling is certainly a skill-based profession. Selling effectively requires learning skills that can be developed. A disciplined approach to selling must be employed by an associate who may be under-performing in a specific performance category which identifies a struggle with a particular area of the experience.

Disciplines and the Customer Experience
So what is the significant difference between a policy, a standard, a best practice and a discipline?

The dictionary defines "policy" as:

pol•i•cy (pol-uh-see)

—noun, plural -cies.

1. a definite course of action adopted for the sake of expediency, facility, etc.: We have a new company policy.

2. a course of action adopted and pursued by a government, ruler, political party, etc.: our nation's foreign policy.

3. action or procedure conforming to or considered with reference to prudence or expediency: It was good policy to consent.

It also defines "standard" as:

stand•ard (stan-derd)

—noun

1. something considered by an authority or by general consent as a basis of comparison; an approved model.

2. an object that is regarded as the usual or most common size or form of its kind: We stock the deluxe models as well as the standards.

3. a rule or principle that is used as a basis for judgment: They tried to establish standards for a new philosophical approach.

4. an average or normal requirement, quality, quantity, level, grade, etc.: His work this week hasn't been up to his usual standard.

5. standards, those morals, ethics, habits, etc., established by authority, custom, or an individual as acceptable: He tried to live up to his father's standards.

Wikipedia describes "best practice" as:

A Best Practice is a technique, method, process, activity, incentive or reward that is believed to be more effective at delivering a particular outcome than any other technique, method, process, etc. The idea is that with proper processes, checks, and testing, a desired outcome can be delivered with fewer problems and unforeseen complications. Best practices can also be defined as the most efficient (least amount of effort) and effective (best results) way of accomplishing a task, based on repeatable procedures that have proven themselves over time for large numbers of people.

But the word "discipline" hits the mark when it comes to describing behavioral consistency for customer experiences because unlike the aforementioned terms, "discipline" is more about a conscious routine for the sake of improvement. The dictionary defines the word "discipline" as

dis•ci•pline [dis-uh-plin]

1. training to act in accordance with rules; drill: military discipline.

2. activity, exercise, or a regimen that develops or improves a skill; training: A daily stint at the typewriter is excellent discipline for a writer.

3. the rigor or training effect of experience, adversity, etc.: the harsh discipline of poverty.

4. behavior in accord with rules of conduct; behavior and order maintained by training and control: good discipline in an army.

When an individual embarks on a mission to change or improve something in their life, it would require having to make a conscious effort of behavioral change until such time that the outcome is natural and instinctive.

- A decision to improve health and fitness requires having discipline around eating and exercise.

- A desire to complete a project would require discipline for time and activity.

Policies, Standards, and Best Practices are words that best describe operational elements that can be easily monitored. Employees show up for work once per day; it's easy to know if they're late. The salesperson is either dressed for work or not. Paper work is complete or incomplete. These don't require a lot of awareness and are easy to enforce as policy. But to enforce a policy on specific elements of the customer experience with every sales presentation is about as easy as getting everyone on the plane to power-down their IPods. And as long as a salesperson is driven by self-intendedness, it's too easy for her to hide in the shadows when a policy occurs at a frequency nearly impossible to observe.

So when it comes to making a decision to provide higher levels of service to our customers, we must make conscious changes to the current service model and/or be more "disciplined" about the consistency required to achieve the goal. In the upcoming chapter on the customer experience, we'll take a further look into specific disciplines for each critical moment in the experience.

Engaging Disciplines that Satisfy the Belief

Customer experience disciplines are those behaviors known to be critical to maximizing each customer experience. They must be delivered consistently to ensure the experience exceeds customer expectations. Customer experience disciplines are those known behaviors that produce the highest desired outcome.

For example, if you were to determine that your current physique needs improvement (you're overweight or out of shape), you would first have to decide what you want your desired outcome to be. Anyone who has experienced a Q&A session with a personal trainer will tell you that one of the first questions asked is, "What are your goals? Is it weight loss or gain, muscle tone or size, stamina or strength?" The answers determine the required routine to achieve the goal. The personal trainer will ask for a "disciplined commitment" from you in order to achieve the highest desired outcome. Should the individual veer from the discipline, the result is compromised. That would be a tremendous waste of time and money.

The purpose of having customer experience disciplines is:

- Ensure that the experience is properly linked to the brand and the company's belief system as to maximize Market Penetration and Customer Share.

- Formalize particular elements of the experience to assure that every customer is served consistently, fully informed of products and specials and given an opportunity to say "yes".

- Have a reference for coaching and developing associates.

It Starts with Customer Readiness

Foundational to an exceptional customer experience is the necessity to prepare the store prior to opening. This means having a store that is ready for business prior to the customer stepping foot into your store. Store readiness requires a commitment to the environment that hosts the experience and has its own set of disciplines. The objective is to create an environment that is "ready" for the customer when they walk through the front door.

In terms of preparing for the fight, it's important to remember that your opponents, the Internet, catalogues and mass merchants, are always perfectly merchandised, priced and perfectly efficient every time the customer visits. So the retail street fighter must level the playing field. Ensuring the in-store experience can rival the competition's method of "readiness" is core to differentiation.

Before the doors open on any given day, the store must be prepared to handle the events (known and unknown) that will occur that day. This is not just the 15 minutes prior to the opening walk through; it's a broader approach to understanding the critical components that ensure customers will have positive first and return visits and a strategy for ensuring customers are served during busy times.

The next time you're on the floor, watch your customers. Notice how they interact with the merchandise. Look at the expressions on their faces when a mechanical or electronic item doesn't work, when a fixture is dirty, when a drawer won't open, and so on. This is how a customer ready store prepares. I'm not talking about the cliché routine of ensuring everyone has an area assigned for clean up and maintenance. This goes beyond seeing the store "with the eyes of a customer". After all, don't customers have 5 senses? So why are retailers only consumed with how the customer sees the store? The mandate is that a customer ready store is aware of how the customer will experience the store, the merchandise and the people hired to serve them. The customer ready store goes beyond store opening checklists and picture books of what a faced off shelf looks like. The customer ready store has" spidie-senses" for how the environment affects the experience. The customer ready store is aware of the processes that require a customer to spend more time than necessary. A customer ready store is in fact, "customer ready".

Customer Ready Disciplines for the Retail Street Fighter.

Creating a customized set of disciplines is a fairly involved process in that it requires mystery shopping, getting customer feedback, interviews with the staff and so on. However, for the sake of providing something you can at least nibble on below is a basic version of some generic disciplines that you can use to bulk up for the street fight. All retailers require customer ready disciplines for operations, staffing and personal readiness. Below are some common ones. When you're ready to get serious and define customer ready disciplines specific to your company…just reach out, call my name, and you know wherever I am (you know the rest).

A CAP Sampling of Operational Disciplines

- The sales floor is clean, merchandised, well lit and music is at an appropriate level and style.

- The climate is conducive for the experience

- The merchandise is positioned for the most common traffic patterns and accommodates your customer base.

- Products that need to move, chime, turn, or hop are operational.

- Price tags are visible, easy to read, and understandable.

- A commitment is made to regularly recover the store physically so customers have a positive impression throughout the day.

- Catalogs and pertinent marketing collateral are staged for new business.

- Merchandise and displays are well kempt and updated and positioned to impact the customer.

- Transactional documents (i.e. order tickets, return/exchange forms, etc) are fully stocked and accessible.

- The backroom is properly set up and staged for receiving, pick-up and return of merchandise.

- The cash-wrap is staged with everything it needs to quickly process a transaction.

A CAP Sampling of Staffing Disciplines

- Store associate skill sets can deliver the disciplines that satisfy beliefs

- There is a proper mix of part timers and full timers according to a staffing census/matrix with scheduling standards for non-busy days and peak traffic time.

- The manager maintains a file of potential candidates for recruitment.

A CAP Sampling of Personal Disciplines

- The staff is dressed within company-approved guidelines regarding dress code, including their name tag.

- The staff is trained on sales, service and product knowledge using the company's learning and development tools.

- The staff employs busy day disciplines for assisting customers efficiently while ensuring new customers are tended to during peak traffic times.

- Awareness of daily and weekly sales goals are provided to ensure the staff is focused on revenue targets.

- Each associate is aware of their personal Performance Improvement Metric as a method for raising their awareness of erosion in the customer experience he/she delivers.

This should give you an idea of how I approach a retailer looking to improve the selling model by setting up the disciplines salespeople need to employ in order to prepare for the customer. Please realize that the customer experience is a learning platform on its own right and can be customized as a workbook, video program and/or seminar for any retailer (plug, plug—I have my own street fight as well). My web site, www.arniecap3.com, can provide more information on it.

Next we'll examine each of the four critical moments of the customer experience and provide context and technique regarding some of the scenarios that can play out within the experience.

The Customer Experience - Simplified

"When a salesperson strives to sell with passion, he is fully intent on the customer's precise and complete needs for the sole purpose of earning customer loyalty."

ArnieCAP

Chapter 6:

The Customer Experience Made Simple

"This chair is too big…this porridge is too cold…this bed is too hard." Today's consumers can be like Goldilocks. Some complain the service they get is too pushy, others feel it's not attentive enough, and they could all be talking about the same store. Some don't even know what it means to be served anymore and have resolved to self-serve as a "type of service". And with a sales force serving customers through the bulk of the day with modest supervision of the experience, it's difficult to bank on consistency. These dynamics, playing out on retail sales floors every day, are why retailers believe that systemic efficiencies are the key to superior customer experiences. Yet I still contend that it's the quality of the experience and diligence to maintain a relationship with customers that makes the experience great and builds loyalty to the brand.

A company truly committed to customers being served beyond their expectations uses customer feedback to define the expectation of the store experience. The use of mystery shopping services, market research and branding experts, focus groups and bounce-back survey vehicles are widely available today; or you can just talk to your customers while shopping or walking to their cars and ask them outright. Either way, you need to know how your customers want to feel while in your store, create context around their expectations, and ensure the store organization is equipped to deliver on the expectations through repetitive training and high awareness of performance trends.

In the selling profession, great salesmanship evolves out of a learning of what works and what doesn't work when attempting to exceed a customer's expectations and close more sales. Out of that learning process a salesperson develops instincts and skills for how to properly build a sale and develop strong relationships with customers. Somewhere along the way, a great salesperson may develop their own method for making sales and it works...for them. In retail selling, the event itself is so destination and desire based that the need for strategically placed technique and well crafted closes may not be as necessary as in those situations where customer need and desire has yet to be established. This point is proven all the time when a rookie salesperson hits a retail floor armed with nothing more than passion and curiosity and somehow gets the register to ring.

Still, higher-touch retail environments and specialty stores with specific product lines that aren't so obvious to the average consumer will always require a degree of salesmanship and certain techniques that turn footprints into a loyal following.

Many don't come to the party with those instincts and skills and if the initial passion and desire runs out of steam, a company must be prepared to address the disciplines and behaviors a salesperson needs to succeed. When a company doesn't have the time to wait for those skills to develop on their own it must provide a roadmap for how to make a strong first impression, build trusting relationships and cause customers to continue the relationship with positive experiences each time they visit the store.

On the street, it is likely you are also going up against other specialty stores within your category. At this level, one might be able to make a pretty good argument over who has the best selection, the best price and even the most knowledgeable staff. Some perceived "advantages" could actually be a bit subjective. However, the one thing that is essentially unmistakably unique is the experience a customer has with an individual working in your store. Customer experiences are a dynamic process. No two experiences are the same because:

a) After a salesperson says "hello," the rest is a completely fluid, unscripted conversation.

b) Other than personal trade clients, a new encounter between a salesperson and a customer is uncharted territory. There's no pre-existing relationship to guide the salesperson on how to engage the customer.

The Roadmap for a Superior Experience

Now that the store is ready for business, there needs to be an understanding of the different types of customer facing scenarios there are and how the staff is expected to serve customers within each of those scenarios. Obviously there could never be scripts for every single scenario that can possible occur; but there are enough similarities within each critical moment that a roadmap for success can be created. For example, the entire experience can be broken down into these critical contact moments:

• Engaging a customer and discovering their expectations

• Revealing product value based on the Buyer's Personal Motivators

• Influencing and maximizing the purchase

• Acquiring contact information and maintaining loyalty to the brand

Within each one of these scenarios are a variety of situations steeped with verbiage and behaviors that promote a positive experience. They are:

• The objective of each scenario

- The customer experience disciplines that underlie the expectation.

- Service enhancements that ensure a consistent and fluid experience

- Tools and collateral materials that help the customer help us

- Techniques, scripts and operational process to aid with consistency

- Busy day and non-busy day strategies

- Handling customer rotation and turnovers within each experience

- Reports and metrics to measure and trend success and help with analyzing performance gaps to coach associates to improve upon these opportunities. These will be discussed in the chapter called "The Story is in the Stats".

When originally charged with the task to simplify sales training, I quickly came to the realization that:

a) Selling is a profession that doesn't require a formal education, ongoing training, or certification. This means salespeople feel they already know what works for them.

b) Salespeople will avoid role-playing at all costs.

c) Training videos with well scripted, ideal scenarios acted out by professional actors are viewed by salespeople as an insult.

d) Anyone worth their salt will fight the request to take time off the floor to go through a long, drawn-out training program.

Because of these constraints, I had to scale back everything I had developed or delivered up to that point to create a Customer Experience Learning Platform that could be used to ramp up new salespeople and coach the struggling ones. It had to be very simple, easy to understand, and quick. And because I firmly believe that selling in retail is not tremendously complicated, then the learning platform shouldn't be either.

Below are sample pages out of The Customer Advocate Playbook that will provide you with a very simple and actionable way to help a struggling salesperson understand your customer experience objectives.

EXPERIENCE 1 - Engage and Discover

Objective - The primary focus is to facilitate an initial impression that helps the customer feel comfortable and welcome. Don't expect that all customers will respond immediately to a charming greeting and an interesting opening line. But as you establish yourself early on as friendly, attentive and interested, you will begin to create an experience that promotes relationship.

Customer Experience Disciplines

- Be attentive to each customer that enters the store.

- Offer a sincere, welcoming greeting that puts them at ease and sets the tone for the relationship.

- Engage the customer with discovery questions that clarify their desires.

Ways to Enhance the Experience

- Allow customers to enter the store and assimilate before greeting them. The greeting should be genuine and the customer approached in a disarming way.

- Stay curious. Use verbal and non-verbal skills to acknowledge your customer's answers, descriptions and stories.

- Attempt to get the customer's name and use it.

- Precisely determine the customer's wants and needs by asking great discovery questions, listening carefully to the answers and thinking about products and merchandise that will exceed their expectations.

- Use store marketing collateral as a tool to get you both on the same page.

EXPERIENCE 2 - The Reveal

Objective - Exceed the customer's needs completely using the full-scope of the product assortment. Build Customer Share and Market Penetration, by merging product attributes with the personal buying motivators learned in discovery. Increase the level of the customer's desire by speaking about the merchandise with passion and engaging the customer in the presentation.

Customer Experience Disciplines

- Merchandise presentations must highlight benefits that are important to the customer.

- Presentations must include appropriate add-ons, accessories, and high-margin enhancements.

Ways to Enhance the Experience

- As the experience unfolds, continue to ask discovery questions to get deeper into the motivators driving the purchase. Reinforce the product attributes that the customer finds valuable.

- Communicate what customers need to know without overwhelming them with jargon.

- Share product knowledge that is relevant. Present those features specific to the customer's expressed needs and preferences.

- Involve the customer in order to confirm the extraordinary quality of the merchandise, so that they understand the tremendous value.

- Begin recommending add on and accessory enhancements.

EXPERIENCE 3 – Influence and Maximize

Objective - Maximize Market Penetration and Customer Share by creating the desire to want and own the products presented, do business with our company and encourage repeat and referral business.

Customer Experience Disciplines
- Ask the customer to buy everything presented that the customer showed interest in.

- Use empathy and additional discovery to resolve any apprehension that may exist and further determine if the customer has budget constraints or value considerations.

- Make sure customers are aware of current promotions and financing options.

Ways to Enhance the Experience
- Be confident in your presentation. Ask for the sale with methods that fit your style and cater to the customer's character traits and personality.

- Continue to recommend product enhancements to ensure the customer is completely satisfied.

- React to verbal and non-verbal buying signals.

- Attempt to overcome product objections or purchase delays with empathy. If a customer seems hesitant or reluctant, use discovery questions and empathy to learn the reason.

- Be solution oriented

EXPERIENCE 4 – Maintain the Relationship

Objective - Maintain a relationship with the customer so that you can provide continued excellent service. We will earn positive word of mouth, the opportunity to serve the customer in the future, and referrals.

Customer Experience Disciplines

- All customers should be asked to join the mailing list.

- Continue the relationship with appropriate callbacks for return, repeat and referral business.

Ways to Enhance the Experience

- Stay in touch with your customers; especially if following up on a purchase delay, or product inquiry.

- Speak in an upbeat and positive manner so that the customer is glad to hear from you (even if you're delivering bad news).

- Thank customers before they leave and ask for referrals.

- Make appointments with phone-in customers and customers who are not ready to buy today.

- Keep a log of customer purchases to build a buying profile as a way to stay in touch when new products arrive.

Other Factors to Consider

Within each of these 4 components of the experience are a multitude of issues and industry specific considerations. Here are a few the retail street fight should address when building their Customer Experience platform:

- Busy day disciplines for efficient transactions when the staff is outnumbered.

- UP or rotation system rules for creating a fair sales floor for each salesperson; minimizing "that was my customer".

- Methods for turning the customer over (TO's) when a salesperson struggles making a connection or maximizing the opportunity and to ensure each customer is being served by a salesperson that best suits their style and expectations.

- Using appointments to control traffic and help scheduling.

- CRM software to build a database of customer purchasing habits and aid with follow up.

Armed with beliefs and disciplines for the fight, the retailer must now begin to develop a sense of what is happening. It would make no sense to have this fight in the dark. Retail street fighters need information, data, and knowledge to identify areas of opportunity. In the CAP Zone, this is known as "awareness".

Developing Awareness— The Story is in the Stats

"Performance trends—self fulfilling prophecies or an opportunity to hold off a disaster? Merchants and marketers cannot react as quickly as a field organization engaged in a micro-focused strategy to flip a down stat caused by behavioral divergence."

ArnieCAP

Chapter 7:

Developing Awareness—The Story is in the Stats

Lately I've been using the word "awareness" a lot. I use it with my kids, I practice it myself, I talk about it with the people I work with and certainly my clients know this word. Awareness, I believe, is one of the greatest life ingredients a person can have. Awareness prevents accidents. Awareness keeps children safe. Awareness protects assets. Awareness is a core element of empathy. Awareness allows you to experience events beyond the four-foot circle around you, and it allows you to help others experience events in their lives as well. Enough spiritual stuff; let's look at the definition to see the literalness behind the word. According to the Encarta Dictionary:

a'ware
Pronunciation [*uh*-**wair**]
—adjective
1. Having knowledge of something from having observed it or been told about it
2. Knowing that something exists because you notice it or realize that it is happening
3. Well-informed about what is going on in the world or about the latest developments in a sphere of activity

Need there be more to say? Beliefs and disciplines are foundational; awareness is actionable. Practicing awareness requires a sense of self, a sense of the environment and a sense of the experiences of those in the environment. Awareness in a retail store is critical to winning the fight and is the essence of customer advocacy. To break down awareness, one would consider the following:

Some questions that should be asked to raise awareness of self:

- What are my personal/store performance goals and minimum performance expectations? How am I doing relative to those benchmarks?

- What statistics do I excel in and why? Are they random or consistent?

- What stats do I/my store struggle with and why? What behaviors would help me improve?

- Is my dress reflective of a professional person? Does my physical appearance have the potential to offend or exclude anyone from wanting to engage with me or respect me?

- How's my product knowledge? Am I versed enough to translate product attributes into Buyer's Personal Motivators.

- Do I know my business well enough that if my supervisor asked me to provide a brief assessment of how I'm doing and what I need to do to improve, will I have an informative response?

Some questions that should be asked to raise awareness of the environment:

- How does the store look? Does it cater to a superior experience?

- Have I walked the store with the expectations of a customer?
- What music is playing and who is it catering to?

If you want to know more about this subject, I highly recommend reading Why We Buy by Paco Underhill. Underhill provides amazing insights into the environmental influences on the customer experience; it is the premier resource on environmental awareness.

Some questions that should be asked to raise awareness of the experiences of others:

- What are my customers doing right now? Are they happy, engaged, enjoying the store?
- Are any customers with the wrong salesperson (bad chemistry, no engagement)?
- Does my staff look ready to serve? Are they aware of what it takes to serve?
- What behaviors should I be working on with Fred or Mary?
- When was the last time I scrimmaged with the staff?
- What do I know about them that would help me help them?

Owners and managers may not have direct contact with every customer that enters the store; they do however bear the ultimate responsibility for the outcome of every customer contact. The more aware of the performance of the individuals who directly serve each customer, the better the chances are of maximizing each and every opportunity.

Where am I?

Where do I want to be?

How will I get there?

These are three basic questions that every retail street fighter must answer if they believe they're responsible and accountable for the performance of the store; or you can continue to blame weather or the economy and hope that things will get better.

Awareness of individual performance is critical. The physical plant itself doesn't actually "do the selling" and tracking store performance alone is not enough. Store performance is only relative to the degree that it provides year-to-year trending, store-to-store comparison, and it helps the pencil pushers forecast EBITDA. Individual associate performance within each store is more activity based than informational. Individual performance provides a manager with a diagnostic tool for identifying "service experience erosion".

Essentially, the manager needs to "SEE" where the customer experience is breaking down without having to watch every single salesperson-to-customer interaction. Through this heightened state of performance awareness, a manager can respond to the behavioral gaps causing the performance deficiency.

Awareness relative to the customer experience essentially considers the following:

- What are my performance expectations?

- What knowledge can I gain from specific performance indicators that point to gaps in the experience?

- How do I best address those gaps?

What are my performance expectations?

Let's begin with establishing performance expectations. There is a significant difference between goal setting and establishing minimum performance benchmarks. Goal setting is not an accountability platform. Let me repeat that; do not use goals as the method by which a person's job is put on the line. Goals are used to inspire and drive higher levels of performance. Goals should be written down and posted when achieved. Goals are used to reward the over-achievers and recognize positive results. It is not the means by which we call attention to poor performance.

In the world of selling, those of us who care know when performance goals are not being achieved. We feel it in our paychecks and see it when results are posted. We don't need our noses rubbed in it. Those who don't care…don't care.

So when retailers ask me how to set up an accountability structure based on setting goals, I quickly refer them to the new vocabulary of retail. The accountability platform for those who consistently under-perform is realized in a term called:

Base Contribution Rate

BCR is the means by which the retail street fighter identifies a level of performance that is not acceptable over a sustained period of time. It can be based on payroll cost percentage, hourly productivity minimums or relative comparisons to store averages in a multitude of statistics. So don't get me wrong, I do believe in performance accountability, I just don't use goal setting at the method.

Before we further define base contribution rate, let's look at methods for goal setting in order to clarify the difference between the two.

There is a multitude of ways to set goals for sales associates. There are just as many terms used to describe goals, such as plans, budgets, benchmarks, targets, etc. Please realize that when setting up a method for goal setting, individual performance objectives should not be subject to a manager's mandate to ensure the store is staffed properly. Here's why:

Understaffed Store:

Manager:	"What happened last month, you missed your goal by 15 percent."
Salesperson:	"Yeah I know, but the store was swamped and I actually made my biggest bonus check so far this year."
Manager:	"I understand, but if you keep missing your goal I'll have to write you up."
Salesperson:	"You gotta be kidding me!"

Overstaffed Store:

Manager:	"Congratulations, you smashed your goal last month!"
Salesperson:	"Are you serious? My Chihuahua could have hit that number. But if I don't start making bonuses, I might have to quit."
Manager:	"Quit? But you're doing so well."

That's why it's important to differentiate between giving someone a goal vs. establishing base contribution rates.

The first element of establishing performance expectations is determining the revenue objective for the store or company. There are quite a few considerations for setting store plans or budgets. Some of the more common are:

- Last year store performance (aka comp)

- Increase in operating expense that affects the breakeven including any department having an increase in their budget

- Promotions held last year, will they occur again and, if so, when?

- Is there going to be a significant difference in marketing (more, less, change in messaging)?

- Will my product buys affect the average ticket or velocity of units sold?

- Economic considerations - I hate this one, but it has to be considered.

- Increase in head count (unless straight commissioned or contracted positions)

- Expansion - more stores could mean higher exposure and more traffic

- Cannibalization - Am I planning a shift in traffic because of a new store opening?

- Weather/external events - Big storm last year shut down the town

- Increased competition - I hate this one too.

So if you are running multiple units, it's extremely important that each store have its own goal, plan or budget. And even if you are a solo street fighter, wouldn't you want to know relative performance to last year or profitability so growth is occurring?

The way store performance planning gets sticky is when determining how the store goal is distributed within the store. I have heard all the arguments about the effects of giving individual performance goals to the staff. Those who do it, swear it has made a significant difference in the overall performance of the store. Those who don't, swear their customer experience is better because there isn't aggressiveness on the sales floor that customers can sense. So who is right?

Goal setting is a must! It absolutely does fuel growth. Where it can get ugly is when it's used as an accountability platform. If salespeople are stressing their jobs are at risk if goals aren't achieved over a certain period of time, then it can get aggressive. That's why I am a firm believer in differentiating between goals and base contribution rates.

Let's begin by breaking down different types of goals setting methods and examining the pros and cons of each.

Individual Trended Performance:

This method is used when individuals have an established performance level in a given time period and the goal or performance objective is based on that known level. This method works if it is being used to "push" the associate to produce higher results for their personal gain. It should not be used as a method for accountability. Therefore this method would be defined as a "goal," not a "base contribution rate". For the store to be successful, the manager would have to ensure the individual goals add up to the store goal or that the store is staffed well enough for the store goal to be achieved. It would be a bummer if everyone hit their goal but the store missed.

Team Performance Objectives:

This method is used when the store owner or manager lets the team know what the store goal is and attempts to hit the mark through group participation or simply divides the store goal up evenly based on a percentage of total productive store hours (all team members hours added up). Again, this is a great way to set a goal, but is not an accountability platform. If the store is understaffed, it may be impossible for the individuals to hit the goal. If there's a particular salesperson that drives a large percentage of the store's performance due to tenure or personal trade, this method may put their goal too low and the others too high.

To summarize, Goal setting is a moving target, I think its necessary, and the retail street fighter can use any method that fits with the business model and staff profile.

Creating a Base Contribution Rate

There are many internal and external influences that affect the salesperson's ability to hit the mark. Goal setting should be the fun part of selling; shooting for the stars, inspiring higher levels of performance, dreaming of getting the new car with the bonus or commission check when blowing away personal objectives.

However, creating an accountability platform for the selling staff requires identifying exactly what is believed to be a minimum level of performance that would cause concern over whether the salesperson can make it on the floor or not. The retail street fighter must first establish the rate of contribution a salesperson must maintain in order to continue serving customers.

Base Contribution Rate and The Customer Experience

In general terms, when a merchant is considering whether a particular product should be reordered or discounted and discontinued from the assortment, the decision is typically based on:

1. Margin Erosion

2. Rate of Turn

3. $ per square foot

If the product does not maintain a minimum level of performance over a sustained period of time, it is subject to elimination from the sales floor. A salesperson's success can be measured in a similar way:

1. Payroll cost percent

2. Productivity rate ($/hr)

3. Sustained performance in the bottom tier of the group.

These are known as base contribution rates. If the salesperson does not maintain a minimum level of sustained performance in any of these categories, he/she is subject to elimination from the sales floor.

Using the aforementioned measurements of salesperson performance, consider the following scenario:

Salesperson Fred makes $10.00 per hour. On a 40-hour week, Fred earns $400.

1. Payroll cost percentage – Let's say a retailer has budgeted a 7.5% payroll cost percent for the selling staff. On this BCR method, Fred would have to sell $5,333.33 to justify his pay. If his sales do not maintain the 7.5 payroll percent, Fred has to take a pay cut, leave the job, or sell more. ($400 ÷ 7.5% = $5,333.33)

2. Productivity rate – Under this format Fred has to have sustained performance of $133.33 per hour in sales to justify his pay or position on the floor. ($5,333.33 ÷ 40 hrs = $133.33/hr)

3. Sustained performance in the bottom tier of the group - This is the one I like. I think the "Biggest Loser" got it right when the contestants are force-ranked within the group and the ones that can't sustain performance above the norms of the group are scrutinized for dismissal. Regardless of performance benchmarks, goals, or other forms for setting revenue objectives, any associate that stays "below the line" on this BCR method (after a given period of time) should be subject to corrective action.

Here is how it works. The chart below shows a group of salespeople.

• The first column is each salesperson's BCR based on how much they need to sell per hour in order to satisfy their 7.5 percent payroll cost of sales.

- The middle column shows their actual sales per hour for the given time period. That time period is relative to your selling cycle. Generally I look at a minimum of 30 days to 3 months to get a solid look at who is carrying their weight.

- The third column identifies the actual payroll cost percent based on their weekly pay.

Salesperson	BCR	Actual	PCR (7.5%)
Emma	$132.67	$190.00	5.24%
Gibson	$133.33	$175.00	5.71%
Sophie	$176.67	$170.00	7.79%
Victoria	$160.00	$162.86	7.37%
Arnie	$133.33	$162.50	6.15%
Total	$149.74	$157.04	7.15%
Kristie	$140.00	$153.33	6.85%
Nic	$170.00	$152.50	8.36%
John	$150.00	$107.14	10.50%

Below the Line Performance

This method of BCR is the only effective way of measuring Top Line performance to goal because it is reflected in the bottom line where it counts. In the scenario above:

1. Sophie is a top performer, but her base pay isn't being justified. She's running a payroll cost percentage of 7.79% which is above the budgeted amount and the store average. Sophie must have sold the owner on a higher rate of pay because of her wonderful résumé and charming interview. She can easily hoodwink the owner or manager

into believing she dominates the sales floor should the store not employ this method of BCR.

2. Kristie isn't costing you payroll and is exceeding her base productivity rate, but she doesn't run with the pack. So this becomes a question of how much time you are willing to work with her to increase her gross sales performance above the store average or benchmark. We would need to find out where she's struggling, but with proper coaching as her sales go up and her payroll cost percent goes down. This is wonderful until she realizes that she makes less than everyone else and asks for a raise.

3. Nic and John shouldn't be serving customers. Their inability to maintain productivity ($/hr), coupled with high payroll cost percentage gets them voted out of the house without losing an ounce of sleep.

By using this method over a sustained period of time, a retail street fighter can quickly identify who should be greeting customers and who should be promoted to customer.

What knowledge can I gain from critical performance measurements that point to gaps in the experiences?

A coach of a sports team wouldn't dream of starting a player without considering his statistics to date. Often coaches base some of their decisions about players on how well they performed against a particular team or opponent at a previous meeting. This is an interesting concept. I wonder what it would do to conversion rate if store managers had insights into which salespeople do better with certain customer types. For example, when David's Bridal began dipping their toe into the prom dress pool, there was clearly a different type of customer shopping for a prom dress than a wedding dress. So although many brides connected with the engaging, involved style of a mature women (like shopping with Mom) Prom girls seemed to prefer huddling within their peer group and didn't want much interference from that same woman. The way the prom customer was engaged and served had to be different and in some cases needed a different style or "type" of salesperson. Store managers needed awareness of this both statistically and experientially so to make the call for the sake of the customer and the store. She had to be aware that a customer experience may go bad if the connection did not occur between a salesperson and her customer.

In many retail stores today store "coaches" manage their associates by emotion, opinion and personal feelings instead of how well they have performed statistically and through awareness on the sales floor. Without base contribution rates and ways to measure performance day to day, week to week, and so on, managers don't really know how well their players are doing. And associates don't know what the manager expects in terms of performance or how well they are doing relative to the job they were hired to do.

Many managers are mostly concerned about whether their associates show up on time or operate the register correctly. But isn't that just a function of their real responsibility, to contribute to the financial growth and profitability of the store? We certainly know that operations can get done routinely and efficiently with a manager who is disciplined about it. But what are the performance expectations for our store associates? What are the benchmarks for whether the store staff is "selling" well or not?

In order to truly know the story of how a salesperson is doing, over time, with a string of customer experiences is to document, track and trend specific performance indicators; ones that point to strengths and opportunities. It would be foolish and irresponsible to react to a situation without gathering all the facts first and taking the time to determine what the facts are saying. Without the facts a person subjectively reacts; with the facts a person can objectively plan and thoughtfully respond. There are countless metaphors available to drive this point home:

- Would a doctor "react" to an illness without running tests and reading a chart?
- Would you take a boat out on the ocean without checking weather patterns first?
- Would you get on a plane that had no gauges?
- Would you select you fantasy football team based on personality and uniform color?

The fact of the matter is this, in order to be clear and decisive about the activities needed to improve the customer experience, the retail street fighter would need to:

1. Realize, regardless of gross revenue performance, there may be an erosion of service in a particular area of the customer experience based on a specific performance indicator.

2. Embark on the following diagnostic process in order to pinpoint the source of the erosion. The process is this:

   a. Identify the statistics that are not trending with company norms or pre-existing benchmarks.

   b. Narrow down the deficiency to the salespeople who are underperforming in that stat.

   c. Determine the behavioral disciplines that can reverse the down stat.

Prior to doing any sort of coaching or training, one has to know where the behavioral opportunities are in the store. From that point, a behavioral strategy can be developed to change the trend and improve the overall performance of the store.

What is Erosion?

One day I asked a group of jewelry salespeople the following question:

"If you make more money this year than you did last year, what would you attribute that to?"

One replied, "It means I sold more," and the rest bobbed their heads in agreement.

"Ok," I replied. "So if you make less money this year than last year, what would you attribute that to?"

The reply, "Less traffic," and the bobbing heads again signifying agreement.

"Hmmm," I muttered. "So if a salesperson makes more money it's because he did a better job of selling and if he makes less, it's the fault of the company and customer?" Furled brows began to appear and I knew I had their attention. Their answers obviously came from the belief that their salesmanship couldn't possibly have gotten worse, so it must be an external issue.

Next I asked, "So what are you working on?" Their faces were blank. They didn't comprehend the nature of the question. So I clarified, "If you needed to make more money, how would you go about doing that?" Again, they insisted that it would require selling more. "Selling more what?" I pressed. "Selling more customers or selling more stuff?" They didn't know definitively. And this, street fighters, is the basis of erosion.

Performance erosion occurs when gaps appear in specific metrics that directly link to specific behavior on the sales floor. It represents an opportunity that, when identified and successfully acted upon create the greatest opportunity to improve the customer experience thus improving revenue performance. It requires more than just a desire to "sell more". It requires pinpoint accuracy for where the erosion is occurring.

Performance gaps appear in two forms:

Informational: Metrics that provide a sense of where performance is going. These are typically statistics that are an outcome of what is happening but not directly caused by a specific behavior. They are typically used for forecasting.

- Dollar volume
- Payroll percent
- Profit margin (Unless you allow discounting)
- Sales per hour
- Corp financial reporting (EBITDA, product turns, etc.)
- Sales per footprint
- Transaction to traffic ratio

Actionable: Metrics that have specific behaviors associated with them that can improve as a result of coaching.

- Average unit price
- Pieces per customer
- Transactions per hour or percent of total
- Service contracts percent
- Accessories ratio

Digging Beneath the Surface

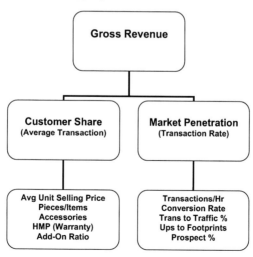

In the chart above it is clear that in order to determine where erosion might be occurring, one must first dig deep past the surface of gross revenue performance and pinpoint areas that have specific behaviors and disciplines associated with them. In order to create growth, a manager must fully understand the metrics used to identify how well the customer experience is being delivered and if there are any inconsistencies in behaviors on the sales floor. When an inconsistency exists, it is revealed in the metrics that exist in the lowest tier.

So, for example, if the store's Customer Share is $1,500 (the average amount per customer purchase) and a particular salesperson is trending at $1,200, it suggests that the salesperson is delivering an experience that causes his customers to spend less than the average customer spends with the average salesperson. To minimize this type of erosion, a manager must first narrow down the performance deficiency and connect the underperforming statistic to the behaviors causing it.

A deficiency in Customer Share suggests the salesperson is struggling with any one or more of the following:

- Average unit selling price – selling higher priced merchandise

- Pieces per customer – adding on merchandise that compliments the primary item or satisfies another need (i.e. a mattress being sold with a coffee table)

- Enhancements – slightly different than adding-on, Enhancements usually consists of smaller, sundry type items that complement the primary item

- HMP – high margin products (i.e. extended service contracts or warranties)

So to coach the salesperson on his personal Customer Share (average ticket) would be a shot in the dark of identifying the behaviors that are causing the erosion. If you look at each of the considerations that affect Customer Share, each has its own set of skills, techniques and disciplines.

To exemplify the sequence, let's say an associate is struggling maintaining their BCR (Base Contribution Rate). Certainly, there is not enough information there for coaching. BCR is nothing more than a flare that suggests erosion in the experience. The only advice for BCR is to sell more. That's like telling Michael Phelps to swim faster.

So now it's a question of Customer Share or Market Penetration. If the associate is getting to the register enough and converting customers at a solid clip, then Market Penetration is ruled out and the erosion is occurring in Customer Share.

Within Customer Share are the specific elements of the experience mentioned above. Lets say in looking at those indicators it is determined the salesperson is struggling selling higher priced items known as AUSP (average unit selling price). The manager would then have the following menu to assist in finding and minimizing the erosion:

Digging for Erosion: Up-Selling
The ability a salesperson has to sell higher ticket merchandise.
- Layer 1 - Total written sales or low BCR
  - Layer 2 - Customer Share (Average Sale)
    - Layer 3 - AUSP
- Behaviors that influence the AUSP:
  - Discovery questions to learn more about the customer and build relationship
  - Product knowledge on higher ticket items to establish value
  - Value building presentations that connect directly to the customer's personal buying motivators
  - Using category coaches (an expert on products the associate struggles with)

Without digging for the exact cause of the erosion, a manager might incorrectly coach a salesperson to close more sales. This would be completely off the mark. A salesperson without the presence of a coach who knows how to pinpoint erosion might conclude that he needs to attempt more add-on. Again, that would not mitigate the deficiency. Average Unit Selling Price is a specific statistic with specific behaviors associated with it. Each of the aforementioned stats has a similar menu. You can go to my Website and shoot me a request from the contact form if you want to learn more.

The final question that must be asked here is, "How long has there been erosion in a particular performance indicator?" Looking at the numbers in weekly increments is not advised unless the plan is to string the weeks together to see trends. A hiccup can occur on any given week and should not be used as the sole means for coaching. And of course the retailer's selling cycle plays into the equation. But for the sake of creating a conclusion to this section, below is a look at a CAP Report that highlights performance over the course of a month.

	BCR	Cust Share	AUSP	PPC	Access%	Trns/Hr	Prspct
August							
Fred	272.59	694.34	471.79	1.47	5.71%	0.39	22.64%
Total	308.37	1014.07	355.81	2.85	17.75%	0.30	57.31%

In this chart, the month of August is shown with some basic performance indicators. Fred is clearly underperforming with BCR. So he is not maintaining his base contribution rate. His Customer Share is where the erosion is happening because his transaction rate is above the store norms (even though he's not prospecting enough—we'll address that later).

Fred's primary deficiency is in adding on. He is not building a ticket (PPC = Pieces Per Customer) and he is not presenting enhancements (Access% = Accessory Percentage).

Fred sells the primary item and moves onto the next customer. Fred is compromising the experiences his customers have in the store and that is not acceptable. Fred's behavior is driven by a belief system that is contrary to his customer's expectations as indicated by the average purchases of other customers in the store. If the average customer spends a grand, why don't Fred's customers.

Fred will want to say that his customers aren't spending like they used to; but the store norms suggest otherwise. You may find that his beliefs are based in the anxiety over being perceived as pushy. Maybe his belief is that he can sell more if he closes the main item and moves onto another customer. That belief would contribute to low rate of sales that come from prospecting. His low prospecting rate suggests that his style of selling also prevents him from building and sustaining relationships and getting referrals. Fred is under-performing in specific performance measurements that tell a story about the erosion occurring in his customer experiences. This is being driven by a belief that is counter to the customer experience. If the belief can be uncovered and replaced by a new belief, Fred will be just fine. If Fred's belief is too strong, there nothing you can do for him. You may get some short-term compliance change, but long-term change can only occur by changing the way Fred thinks.

No retail street fighter can ever maximize the opportunity with Fred in their corner if he's dug his heels in with a strong counter belief about adding-on and/or prospecting. It's been said that if your expectations are not being met, immediately lower your expectations. This will become a reality if Fred's performance and the gaps in the experiences he delivers are ignored, rationalized, or dismissed.

What happens next is that Fred and his manager must have a performance improvement meeting. This one-on-one get together is an opportunity for the manager to assist Fred with understanding where erosion is occurring, link the erosion to behaviors within the customer experience, and attempt to reveal any counter-beliefs he may have that is driving the behavior.

Performance Improvement Meetings

When having a formal session to review performance, there is a very simple premise that has to be considered; a person is his or her own best authority and in general, salespeople are very self-intended. So asking them to buy in, think like an owner or become a team player, although motivational, may not hit the right buttons. Helping people discover how to improve their performance and increase their earnings will speak directly to their desire to earn more. The task is to enable people to discover their own internal scaffolding, their own resources, as the means of finding a resolution to their performance deficiency. Remember that when you give advice and it goes wrong, there will be only one person to blame. You!

Consider the following:

Brenda is a six-year veteran salesperson who has always been a steady performer. She is also very friendly, personable and doesn't "rock the boat" on the floor. Since tracking her sales performance, you've noticed that she underperforms with selling extended warranties more often than not. Her gross sales are solid, her average ticket and conversion rate are right in the mix, but HMP (high margin products) isn't where it should be.

- What are Brenda's beliefs about HMP? Are they consistent with the company's beliefs?

- If Brenda has a counter-belief is it creating behaviors that compromise the customer experience?

- Are there external influences that might be causing the deficiency?

- What will Brenda's reaction be when she is targeted for improvement?

- What do you know about Brenda that would help her understand why improving this statistic is important? How have you helped Brenda in the past?

It is quite common for the supervisor to sit with a salesperson and provide direct information about how to improve. This style tends to be self-serving and generally unproductive. First of all, if there is only direction with no consequences or no teeth in the consequences, the salesperson will nod their head in agreement and try to get through the meeting without bringing up lunch. If the advice doesn't work (or he claims it didn't work), then the manager is on the hook for the advice. Remember, most managers don't have the luxury of watching enough sales presentations to truly know if behavior is changing. So the manager has to wait for the next meeting to see if change occurred; if it didn't, the manager often continues to "tell" the salesperson how to improve; and the cycle continues.

Instead, the manager should hold back the "normal reactions," to give advice and instruct to enable the associate to identify with their belief system and find ways within their selling style to reverse the performance deficiency. When the salesperson creates their solution, she's then on the hook for the expected improvement.

Taking another couple of pages out of The Customer Advocate Playbook, below is a typical process for having a performance improvement meeting with a salesperson.

Conducting a Performance Improvement Meeting

Preparation is critical. There is no way a manager can address performance improvement without the facts and stats.

- Review the CAP reports and validate strengths and performance improvements. Comprehend the implications of the data—establish connections between different metrics and the results.

- Identify categories with the most opportunity for improvement.

- Pinpoint actionable performance gaps within those areas.

- Draw preliminary conclusions about the possible root causes of these gaps.

- Observe behaviors prior to your meeting to identify potential root causes of performance gaps.

Identify and Target. Show the salesperson the CAP reports. See if he/she can identify a performance gap.

- Set up each meeting by making the salesperson feel comfortable.

- Don't dominate the conversation. You learn more by asking questions.

- Create self-discovery. A person is more likely to change behavior based on personally identifying with the opportunity to improve than being told about the opportunity and instructed on how to correct their behavior. Use discovery questions to cause the salesperson to reveal the disciplines, behaviors, skills and techniques that require consistent execution in order to realize performance improvement. Guide them if they are struggling with this, but avoid giving them the answers.

- Don't accept responses like:

  - My customers don't…

  - I can't role play.

  - I'm better with real customers.

- Don't get derailed. Focus on real behavioral change, not attitude.

- Confirm understanding of performance expectation and the underlying beliefs that drive behavior.

- Establish performance expectations for a statistic that would have the greatest impact on performance and improve the customer experience. Show the impact it will have on overall performance and potential commissions

Agree on a Plan. Agreement is crucial. Anything less than a convincing reaction to the behavioral strategy is an indication of a counter belief that has not been revealed.

- Uncover any counter-beliefs or perceived constraints that may get in the way of growth and change.

- Confirm understanding of performance expectation and the underlying beliefs that drive behavior.

- Identify specific actions that must be carried out to close performance gaps.

- Choose learning priorities that when acted upon successfully, will enable the salesperson to close existing performance gaps.

- Devise a logical, effective action plan focused on behavior modification—list actions that are specific, measurable, actionable, realistic and time-bound.

- Stick with a gap that can cause sustainable improvement.

Initiate the skill development process. Words can't move mountains. This meeting serves as nothing more than a reference point for the learning and development that needs to occur on the floor.

- Get on the floor with the salesperson and initiate learning through scrimmaging activities that will assist with the salesperson's development.

- Verify during the week that the desired behaviors are being displayed.

Create a method to track growth. The last thing you want is to have the week go by without knowing if change is occurring. The salesperson must be required to track the performance deficiency during the week and provide daily status updates back to the manager.

- Monitor performance results on an ongoing basis.

- Ensure the salesperson understands how to gauge performance during the week by simplifying a tracking method.

  - "In order to improve your conversion rate from 25 to 28 percent, you will need to close nearly two out of seven UPs. So if you have served five customers and haven't closed one, the burden is to close the next two to avoid having to close four out of the next seven."

- Check progress during the week.

- Follow up at the next session.

Unless a salesperson has absolutely no experience selling and the meeting has turned into skill development, chances are the salesperson knows what to do; they are just avoiding it or have a belief that is creating the deficient behavior. Questions drive solutions, statements and lectures on selling aren't sustainable.

So let's review where we are:

- There's a retail street fight occurring and the winner gets the customer.

- The retail street fighter has to find their passion to serve as the fuel for success.

- A belief system is needed to enlist the behaviors and actions necessary to respond to the customer's expectations.

- Fighters need to be disciplined and consistent in order to maximize their chance of winning.

- Awareness is critical. The retail street fighter must be armed with information about himself, his opponent and the arena where the fight will occur.

So let the fight begin. The next chapter stresses the need for a supervised sales floor. This becomes the stage for customer advocacy. It's the place where beliefs, discipline and awareness collide. It requires a commitment to the philosophy that every customer counts.

Taking it to the Street

"Success is not sustainable
without repetition."

ArnieCAP

Chapter 8:

Taking it to the Street

Somewhere in a retail store today, a customer is being:

- Ignored

- Dropped

- Short-served (not added on to)

- Walked

- Poorly switched

- Influenced by an unkempt environment

- Left in the dark (poor communication/follow-up)

- Forced into a relationship with a salesperson she can't connect with

These are not necessarily compliance issues; they actually represent opportunities to be an advocate for the customer. In all of my travels, in every speech, seminar and presentation delivered, I run into owners and managers wanting to hang their salespeople out to dry because of poor attitude or lack of ambition or less than stellar mystery shopping reports. And in each one of these situations, I've wanted to grab the manager by the back of the collar and say to them, "Are you kidding me? This is your fault, not theirs. The only reason this is happening is because you're letting it; you're allowing it."

Consider this metaphor:

I often go to the zoo and when I do, something very interesting happens. When I look into the lion's den, the lions are doing what lions do. When I visit the panda exhibit, the pandas are doing what pandas do. When I observe the monkey cage, you get the idea?

When I visit different malls around the country I tend to find the exact same phenomenon. When I walk by the Hallmark store, the associates are behind the cash register or replenishing stock. When I walk by The Gap, the associates are folding shirts, opening dressing rooms and running the cash register. When I walk by a Build-A-Bear, the associates are staged for the process; greeting customers and helping children pull the heartstrings of their parents (which are connected to their purse strings). In other words, the mall is the human zoo. Just stroll down the main thoroughfare and watch the humans behave. If a particular cage seems interesting to you, walk up and press your face against the window. One of the humans might look your way, tilt their head in a curious, pensive manner, and then go back to the activity at hand.

The only difference is that if you put a lion in the monkey cage, the lion will still behave like a lion. But, if an associate of a Hallmark store, who tends to be more involved in merchandising and transacting, was moved to the Build-A-Bear store, the associate would evolve to match the spirit and behavioral tendencies of the store. The point being that the associate is looking to fit in, be lead and managed and will morph into a new employee; one that may often be completely different than what they were under previous employment.

Behavioral consistency, service delivery and superior customer experiences are facilitated by the beliefs, disciplines, awareness and commitment of the leadership of the organization. It's cultural. It's not the salespeople who are at fault if customers aren't being greeted or added-on to if there's no message or no one driving it. These big brand companies mentioned above, in essence, have branded their experience. Each Gap around the country behaves fairly consistently. The associates assist customers moving through a brand driven by merchandise and marketing. This is who they are and this is what the customer has come to expect from the experience. Could they deliver higher-touch service? I suppose they could, if that's what they wanted. I am quite sure that if The Gap wanted to provide a more service centric experience, it would just be a matter of choosing to do so.

An independent retailer that doesn't have the brand power of these aforementioned companies must work at this point to establish their particular service model; in essence, brand the experience. If the indie brick and mortar store does not provide a compelling reason for the customer to be loyal to that store, the customer will default to price and service efficiency. The only way to combat that is by delivering an experiential difference that has to be facilitated and materialized. How should your associates behave and what messaging will be required to ensure the experience is consistent?

Behavioral consistency with the customer experience is more of an objective than an activity. Creating core beliefs, defining customer experience disciplines and developing awareness all lead to more consistency with each customer. But consistent behavior and performance cannot be self-managed. It requires having someone who "cares" about the customer and committed to the idea that every customer counts. This person ensures that each customer is being served to the degree that the beliefs and disciplines are being realized.

Sales management must evolve to a position known as customer advocate. This is no different than when Disney started a buzz when they began to call their customers "guests" and their associates "cast members". This decision was a beautifully orchestrated move to identify the position with the brand and the experience.

A customer advocate is the person who ultimately ensures that beliefs, disciplines and awareness are top-of-mind with anyone who has face-time with customers. The title becomes more synonymous with the responsibility of the person in the role. Oftentimes, managers are asked to think like an owner when it comes to running a store or serving customers. Terms like "entrepreneurialism" are used as a way to motivate managers to think on their feet and be responsible for outcomes. But this is not a realistic expectation because the manager doesn't have ownership. He can't empathize because he doesn't have the burden of making payroll, keeping the banks and lenders happy, making payments on leases and other operating costs, etc.

What he can control and impact is how a customer is treated and if the service provided exceeds the customer's expectations as well as the top and bottom line performance objectives for the store. As core beliefs, disciplines and performance objectives become common elements of the store or company, the staff will come to understand that they are not "suggestive;" they are the way to deliver service excellence beyond the expectations of each and every customer and achieve the consistency that is critical to the fight.

In the movie Sliding Doors, the character played by Gwyneth Paltrow embarked on dual parallel storylines that unfolded in different directions based on a split-second incident. The metaphorical hiccup sent her character down two completely different roads and life experiences. In a store, the difference between customers receiving a superior experience by Mary vs. a lackluster experience by Fred could be nothing more than Mary being distracted for a millisecond as the customer enters the store. In most retail stores today, management is not aware enough to notice this and if they are, would most likely not have the wherewithal to intercede or know why they should. And if Fred doesn't close the sale, the manager should go and ask him, "If Mary had that customer, is it possible an item would have been sold?" In most cases, the "Freds" of the world will strongly believe that if he couldn't have sold the customer, no one could have. This line of thinking completely violates everything I know to be true about the profession known as sales.

If Fred's logic were true, wouldn't all salespeople essentially perform the same within a relative time period? If Fred's logic were sound, then he is implying that salesmanship is bogus and that all sales are driven by the customer, not by the experience provided by the salesperson. Meaning that even if the customer has a terrible experience, the need for the item will drive the purchase even if the customer can get it elsewhere. This is just insane and any salesperson who believes otherwise is going to get their clock cleaned in the street fight. There may have been a time when the experience didn't matter as much because value-oriented pricing drove the decision. But with so many channels available to the consumer to get incredible pricing without being abused, those days are all but gone.

But if a manager were on the floor being the customer advocate, he/she might have noticed that this customer seemed disengaged and isn't responding to Fred's attempt at being charming. The customer advocate might assess that Mary's more straightforward style is more appealing to this particular customer than Fred's informal style. The customer advocate would be aware that Fred has as lower transaction rate than Mary and he's about to perpetuate it. The customer advocate would care about this customer and would be committed to the company's objectives and expectations and would take the necessary steps to ensure this customer experiences the store well.

If the spirit of customer advocacy were a full-time position in a retail store, then there wouldn't even be a need for an "UP" or rotation system. Now for those of you who have labored through the process of implementing a way to rotate your salespeople (many of you on my counsel), don't slam the book closed and completely write this chapter off; hear me out. Remember, this book is about creating superior customer experiences that meet and exceed customer expectations. And this chapter is about facilitating superior customer experiences as a management directive. The term "customer advocate" is represented as a new paradigm and alternate nomenclature to the old standard once known as sales management. So the first question I have to ask is this, "Do you care about your customers and how they experience your store?" Yes? Please read on.

Next question: "Is it possible that a customer's level of desire to buy might be diminished if she can't identify with, or actually like the associate "next in line" to serve her? Hmmm. If you are inclined to say "yes," here as well (and you know you are, after all, do you like everyone you meet?), then you should strongly consider conceptually what you are about to read.

Who are we as specialty retailers? Are we the Department of Motor Vehicles, where you get the next agent and subsequently are forced into trying to get them to be empathetic to us? And what choice do we have? It's not like you can use the competitive DMV in the next strip center down the street.

If the ultimate performance objective is to increase the number of transactions and shopper conversions, as well as the size of each transaction, then the customer advocate's role would be to create an experience most likely to satisfy those objectives. That experience not only has to be environmental, but also has to be experiential.

This epiphany became painfully clear to me one cold, rainy night at a rental car counter at Chicago's O'Hare Airport. After being told that the company's express rental service was closed after 10 p.m., I had to stand in line behind four people waiting to get my car that I had reserved through my express rental account with that company.

While standing in line, a huge banner was hanging in front of me that screamed, "Why wait in line when you can express rent with…?" This was the same question I was pondering. There were three agents behind the counter and one in particular that I thought might not have been too happy to be there. As I moved closer in line, the inevitable seemed clear, the unhappy agent would become mine.

So, after waiting in line, when I knew I shouldn't have been, staring at a marketing message that was clearly a lie, I heard the words that would haunt me forever; "Next."

My initial thought was to say, "No thanks, I'll just wait for one of the other agents to free up. You appear to be off your game and I'm slightly peeved as well. I don't think this is a good match." My actually thought sounded more like a Joe Pesci character, but you get the idea.

As I stepped up to the agent, I mustered up the energy to ask why the sign was hanging. Wouldn't it make more sense to take it down after 10 p.m.?

She didn't take well to the query and said she would take it up with management. She then proceeded to give me a car in the last spot of the last row of the lot; and remember it was raining.

As I drove to my hotel, I pondered the experience. Why is it that I had to take the next agent in line? Why didn't I have the huevos rancheros to speak up? Why was I forced into this relationship? And then I realized that the "UP" system I have been implementing in retail stores for years is no different. The "UP" system forces a customer into a relationship with the next salesperson in line. Not a problem if that salesperson can develop affinity with every human being met or has the guts to turn the customer over if not engaging; but not likely.

So how does this get managed? The answer lies in the fact that a customer advocate would have to use awareness through observation and through statistical analysis to know which salespeople need help assessing customers for the sake of engaging them properly and which ones need to know how to step out when the experience is less than the expectation of the customer.

Go ahead, have the "UP" system; just make sure it's being managed for the sake of the customer. Many companies I have worked with track "UPs" using a manual tracking system for rotating the salespeople through traffic. Some even use systemic programs. What I don't see is an "UP" system that tracks information about the types of customers a particular salesperson struggles with. If we go back to the example of Fred and Mary, it might be interesting to know if Fred always struggles with that customer profile. This would be very important in a company that believes every customer counts. Because if, in fact, Fred struggles with that customer type and on a given Wednesday when the store is slow and every dollar matters, Fred is up when that customer type comes in, the customer advocate would be on high alert if Fred is bombing. The customer advocate would page Fred by saying, "Fred, Mary is on line one." This is the customer advocate's secret code to Fred that Mary should take that customer.

Now, make all the arguments you want about split sales and fairness on the sales floor and "that's my up" and all the other self-serving spew meant to protect sales people. I care about all of, but not at the expense of the customer. The seminar about this book called "Every Customer Counts" provides very specific rules about how to handle customer rotation, split sales, and the difference between a volunteer turn over and a management turn over. But nothing is ever more important than the customer experience and that, my fellow street fighters, is how to snatch a customer out of the market and build loyalty to the brand; play match maker on the sales floor and watch the register ring.

Imagine a customer advocate knowing exactly which customer types Fred struggles with and how that information would provide the basis for coaching and scrimmaging. Imagine the possibilities.

Being The Customer Advocate

Having the ability to get the most out of another human being is not something that comes naturally for most people. In fact, many managers are chosen because they are responsible and loyal. Having the qualities to lead and draw the best out of people is often easier said than done. The reality is that every quality a person possesses has underlying skills and abilities that cause the quality to develop. Some of the qualities may already be there, while others may take some time to develop. The key here is keeping top-of-mind, the qualities that aren't natural. They may be qualities that you have to develop and hone, so that as you develop your skills, the qualities become more natural.

For example, when someone trains to be a scuba diver, much of that training is centered on what to do in an emergency. If you were frightened on the ground, the natural reaction might be to hold your breath and run. However, if you were frightened under water and frantically swam to the surface holding your breath, your lungs could burst! So in scuba diving, the training is about purposeful development of new instincts and resisting you natural inclination to surface immediately.

Similarly, the development of behavior in your staff may require not doing what your normal reaction or response might be and putting aside instincts to tell, instruct or demand. If long-term skill development is the objective, it requires learning how to go deeper with a person as opposed to drifting along the surface. This process can help the salesperson find the answers to their own performance deficiencies.

Coaching is not necessarily about demanding compliance, which is often a natural response. However it is about resisting the natural instinct to instruct and replacing it with appropriate guidance on the sales floor. And like the scuba diver, it is imperative to stay focused and facilitate self-discovery even though we may feel the need to instruct. When you instruct others to behave in a particular way, or tell them what to do, or try to fix something for them, you might weaken their natural ability to resolve their own difficulties and create behavior out of fear and compliance rather than beliefs and desire.

This may come back to haunt you because providing solutions makes you responsible for the outcome. Short-term compliance certainly has its place. It's quite necessary when it comes to policy violation and corrective action; but long-term, developmental and sustainable growth comes from guiding people towards seeing performance opportunities and helping them find within themselves the behaviors that promote performance growth.

The Power of Propaganda

In the absence of a full-time customer advocate, there are ways a retail street fighter can ensure the staff is getting the message. There needs to be a propaganda machine at work at all times. Signs, bulletins, reminders, morning meetings, scrimmaging and anything else you can think of to let the staff know what your expectations are. Although the next chapter discusses staffing for the experience, I'll mention here that your new recruits should be run over by the propaganda machine from day one.

Here are ways to oil the machine:

- Consistently reinforce the customer experience disciplines and any other behaviors that enhance the experience.

- Have strategically placed "messaging" in view for all store associates, keeping them constantly aware of and in touch with the company's beliefs, standards and performance objectives.

- Look for gaps in the experience through analysis of key performance indicators on the CAP reports.

- Consistently look for opportunities to coach and develop associates with ways to improve the experience.

- Use your time wisely when meeting with your staff. The first 10 minutes of every store meeting should be a **belief awareness moment** (BAM!).

- Make yourself aware of what customers are saying and feeling.

- Every store associate should be able to express and communicate their core beliefs.

Scrimmaging - The Key to Consistency

If you recall from the previous chapter on awareness, I made mention of the TV show The Biggest Loser. Have you ever watched this masterpiece? What an inspiration. So not only do they have the right perspective on substandard performance outcomes, but they also know how to ensure that everyone gets a fighting chance to win. Can you imagine what the results of the people on that show would be if they had no Jillian or Bob pushing them? Sometimes show contestants are released from the show and can manage to keep things going on their own. But that is only after they have been immersed in a new belief system, received a disciplined approach to health and fitness, created an awareness of progress and stayed committed to the cause. Sound familiar?

Jillian and Bob push these people to the extreme of what is thought impossible. The contestants swear at them, puke, walk away and threaten to quit. Does this stop Jillian and Bob? Not for a second. They're not there to win a popularity contest; they are there to push these people to achieve what is truly desired deep inside them.

The behaviors to achieve the outcomes are known, but Bob and Jillian breathe life into them and create a new belief. And in the end there's a lot of love in the room and a lot of tears from the contestants who feel they let their trainer down.

The customer advocate's role is to do this very thing. Drive people, drill them, push them past their resistance points, point out their flaws and draw out the known solutions.

Scrimmaging plays a significant part in reinforcing the core beliefs and customer experience disciplines. Some retail organizations put a lot of emphasis on sales training while others only scratch the surface. However, if you're not going to hold your teams accountable for sales performance objectives, then why should they be motivated to learn how to sell more effectively?

The reason to scrimmage is simple; it improves the behaviors, skills, and confidence that underlie the customer experience, which, in turn, closes performance gaps. Professional athletes do it, pilots use flight simulators, attorneys have mock trials, actors have dress rehearsal, so certainly retail salespeople can role-play! Still not convinced scrimmaging is necessary? Ask yourself these two simple questions:

- Do I believe I can affect and change the course of my store's current performance?

- Am I willing to hold my associates accountable for base contribution rates?

- If the answer is yes, then you must scrimmage to know how to accomplish this. If the answer is no, then specialty retail may not be for you.

Scrimmaging Defined

The only valid measure of the effectiveness of learning and developing selling skills is the ability of the salesperson to apply experience disciplines with every customer and apply them well enough to increase sales. It's not just a matter of teaching techniques. It's a matter of getting salespeople to recognize the value in consistent and disciplined behaviors on the floor so not only are they capable of executing them, but they want to use them. Scrimmaging helps them break through the mundane life of waiting for the next "good up".

Scrimmaging is a customer experience mock up for a behavioral modification tied to a performance gap. It requires interaction between two or more people where each person is assigned a role. Each person is given a general outline of a situation in which to react and actions are unrestrictive.

There are several reasons why you as a leader should scrimmage as a regular part of your learning platform:

- It's active and interactive.

- It allows an employee to reveal their personal style.

- It allows employees the opportunity to develop new skills without practicing on customers.

- It may help employees identify with "real world" situations.

- It reinforces the company's beliefs and disciplines.

- It improves the employees' comfort level and confidence in using key selling techniques.

There are many ways to use scrimmaging as a learning experience for store associates, including:

- To present new information/skills: A prepared scrimmage can be a very powerful way of imparting information. For example, the impact of a new discipline or behavior can be demonstrated with an associate asking questions that other associates will likely ask. This will prevent repetition and ensure consistent messaging.

- To enforce a model behavior: A scrimmage can be a demonstration of a preferred behavior that can be emulated. Examples might be appropriate greeting of a customer, how to build a ticket or dealing with a customer complaint.

- To rehearse: Scrimmaging can provide the opportunity to build confidence, practice an approach to a situation that one is about to face, practicing a behavior before using it "for real" on the customer, or working out a "trouble spot".

- To enhance self-awareness and sensitivity: Exposure to feedback and the views of others can help to modify one's behavior by providing an insight into its effects on others.

There are some very essential qualities to scrimmaging that help in the leaning process. They are:

- Maintain a positive environment: When scrimmaging, it's important for salespeople to feel safe about the experience. Don't use role-plays that set them up to fail. Keep the interaction upbeat and positive.

- Define your performance and behavioral expectations: Salespeople can only go so far on "self-management". As the customer advocate, ensure that the team is fully aware of what is expected.

- Transcend their beliefs: Before any behavioral change can occur, first uncover the salesperson's personal beliefs about what you are trying to help them with. Once their belief system is revealed, you can help guide them toward aligning their beliefs with the company's.

- Discover strengths: Although we don't want to give mixed messages, it is important to call out positive attributes the salesperson has. This helps keep those behaviors strong while working on others. Asking questions causes them to have to find the answers and be responsible for them.

- Be reliable: When you make arrangements to meet with someone to work with them and commit to the meeting, avoid being interrupted, pulled away, and unfocused.

- Respect confidentiality: To be respected, you must provide respect. Unless you are engaging in group scrimmaging, whatever you are working on with a particular salesperson should stay between the two of you.

- Maintain boundaries: It is extremely important that you do not let your personal feelings about a salesperson compromise your need to help them improve.

In the Every Customer Counts seminar, we go into great detail about how to scrimmage and even set up of few mock scenarios to help develop those skills.

I think I'll end this chapter with one of my favorite customer advocate drills called "lucky day". I got this idea from one of my Ashley Furniture customer advocates. Every day, he assigns a "lucky day" to a particular salesperson. This means that the customer advocate gets prepared for the day by learning everything needed for that particular salesperson. The customer advocate reviews previous coaching docs, performance trends and stats, prepares quizzes and anything else that arms him with information. Then for the entire day, the customer advocate hangs with that salesperson. The entire day is spent coaching, scrimmaging, quizzing, taking turn-overs and reviewing sales presentations; all done in the spirit of pushing the person to learn. The manager essentially becomes the salesperson's "spotter"; being there to push the salesperson past their perceived limitations and validate their potential. Obviously, this is done with a great deal of fun and though this may be reserved for lower tier performers, should not be viewed as punitive. But make no mistake, all the salespeople are inclined to want to keep their chops up in case tomorrow is their "lucky day".

On the final page of this chapter is the customer advocate's creed. Feel free to tear it out of the book and post it anywhere necessary to be reminded of your mission to ensure every customer counts.

The fight for the customer is done on the sales floor. The degree of advocacy for the customer experience may very well determine who gets the prize—customer loyalty.

The Customer Advocate's Creed

1. I commit to ensuring the discipline for delivering superior shopping experiences is consistent throughout the organization that has been entrusted to me.

2. I will realize this through diligence to operational efficiency, relentless communication of beliefs and customer disciplines and a high degree of awareness and responsibility for revenue performance and sustained profitability.

3. I will provide an unrelenting commitment to the ongoing development of the very people I hired to engage the customer.

Staffing
The Experience

"A successful store organization is one committed to ensuring the discipline for delivering superior shopping experiences is consistent throughout the company. This requires an unrelenting dedication to the ongoing development of the very people who were hired to engage the customer."

ArnieCAP

Chapter 9:

Staffing The Experience

For decades retailers have been expressing to me their frustration with compliance issues. They site poor attitude, a lack of motivation, not taking ownership and a myriad of other accountability and willingness issues as the culprit. If one were to explore these factors, it would be quickly realized that these are actually symptoms, not causes. Everyone working in your store today passed an interview. So either the interviewer was completely inept, or the interview was just fine and the system the person was hired into turned a good person bad.

My experience is that most people getting hired today are well intended to do good work, be responsible and, at some level, satisfy the obligations of the job they are being paid for. Even people who have no intention of making a career in retail can provide wonderful experiences to a customer and the company they work for, no matter how short-lived their desire to work for you may be. So how is it that we find our stores filled with poor attitudes, low motivation and a lack of accountability and willingness?

The answer to this question is found in the previous eight chapters of this book. So if, for some strange reason, you found yourself drawn to this chapter initially and decided to read it first, then chances are you are either in the throws of being understaffed, have had random success with your recruiting and hiring efforts, or you can't seem to figure out why the people who turned you on in an interview are suddenly driving you nuts. So you've jumped to this chapter hoping to find some hint of hope. A great employee experience, one that is mutually gratifying, begins with the environment and the culture of the organization being hired into.

I have been saying for years that interviewing is like dating; you really don't know a person until you've lived with them for a while. So the issue behind building a great staff is contingent on the notion that the person who dazzled you in the interview is the same person that shows up for work everyday.

The essence of this chapter is not necessarily about the latest recruiting techniques or insights to human resource issues; I leave those topics to the experts. The objective is more about creating an experience for employees that help your efforts in fueling their belief in you, your customer experience and the company.

The Employee Experience and The Customer Experience

So how does a retail street fighter find people who share their passion to serve? They're out there. Sometimes you've experienced them yourself while shopping and didn't even realize it. I have found people who proved out to be wonderful in spite of the fact they delivered a lackluster experience to me while I was shopping. This is because I see the poor experience for what it is. Is it the person or the company she works for? My technique is to engage them and get them talking to me. I turn into the dream customer. And although this "set-up" may not reflect a typical customer, the scenario acts as a catalyst for her belief system so her style of service will come through.

But most high-touch retailers would never experience this if the associate is guilty by employment. If the company she works for doesn't have the accountability structure in place to insist on that level of service, she's may not be inclined to deliver it. But it may be there; it's just the current employer hasn't tapped into it. And regardless of if I'm actually recruiting or just chumming for names, a few simple questions about who she is, what she wants out of life, and how she feels about the company can quickly reveal the level of passion buried deep inside.

What is often found when I draw a person out like that is the individual works in a company that doesn't provide expectations, doesn't fuel the human spirit, doesn't have fun, doesn't provide objective and developmental feedback and thus, it breaks the spirit of the employee. Even the most passionate employee can't fight against that kind of culture. So the once passionate person, who showed up to the interview, repays the employer by turning an uninspired employee experience into an uninspired customer experience.

The delusional response to that would be, "Well, if she's that unhappy, why wouldn't she quit?" Because it's her job, the way she makes a living, the way she pays her bills. Because the devil she knows is better than the one she doesn't. She doesn't want to update her résumé and hit the street looking for a new job. She knows how prospective employers react to an unemployed person who wants to blame her previous boss for the reason she quit. She's gotten used to the fly by comments her boss calls feedback and other than being verbally spanked every once in awhile, she can deal with the rest.

So even if your point of view is that you have the right to insist she do things a specific way because you're paying her, unless your plan is to get only enough out of her to satisfy that objective at a minimal level, then she will require an environment that provides equal parts of inspiration and structure to go beyond the minimum.

Some candidates I've interviewed felt it was the employer who portrayed an incredible work environment only to find it was more of a marketing ploy to fill the position than a reality. It could have been an out-of-touch recruiter who hadn't spent a day working in the store. So the enthusiastic employee finds within short order that the company touting fun and standards and growth and training and objective accountability in reality is unfocused, lacks standards, uses subjective and vague coaching and doesn't actually practice what is preached.

At many seminars I've conducted, attendees were asked if they've ever felt like wiping out the entire staff and starting from scratch. We marveled over how many people identified with that. If you ponder that question carefully, it's not hard to conclude that if an entire group of people is causing such distress, then it's more likely the environment and system than the people. Sorry, but that's the fact.

It makes you wonder:

- Did the employees let down the company or did the company let down the employees?

- Is it actually possible that every employee was just a fox in sheep's clothing when interviewed?

- Are the interviews so hapless that it doesn't vet out candidates as being a wrong fit before becoming employees?

- Is the manager so desperate that interviews become mechanical and warm bodies are hired?

These can be rhetorical questions or you can use them to challenge your next round of interviews. The bottom line is this, when the culture is alive in an organization and people are happy to be there and feel like there's good exchange of pay and work experiences for the expectations of the job, then it's quite easy to pinpoint someone who isn't a fit or doesn't share the company's beliefs about serving others. But if your candidates are coming in as grapes and turning into raisins, it's more environmental. There is only so much even the most enthusiastic candidate can do when dropped into an environment that doesn't nurture and cultivate their enthusiasm.

Finding Passion

There's a lot of material and seminars out there on recruiting. And as I said, I don't need to make an attempt to provide you with something new, when the existing methods are just fine. But when it comes to recruiting, what I can offer you is this:

- Don't' ever stop looking for new associates – Even if you absolutely have no spot available, you should be in a constant state of building a bank of potential candidates that you can plug in at anytime. A merchant never stops looking for products that have great potential to sell. A manager should have that same consideration about people. What you want is a robust Rolodex of people you can call should a spot open up. You may just catch a person who recently had words with a supervisor and is ready for something new.

- Create a web - Even a person who isn't quite right for your store probably knows somebody who is. Don't stop talking with a person just because they may not be the right candidate for your company. Remember, there are only six degrees of separation between you and Kevin Bacon. I'm sure there's a great employee somewhere in between.

- Be the mayor of the mall – In a mall? Near a mall? Everyone should know you and where you work. Tell anybody who will listen that you have a great employee experience (provided you do). Become the American Idol of retailing. You want as many people showing up as possible.

- Exchange names with another retailer who may have a different service model than you. You have a high-touch jewelry store. Eric has an enthusiast-based vintage record shop. One day a person comes into your jewelry store looking for a job. The interview doesn't pan out based on her lack of experience with high-end stones. But during the interview, she starts talking about things she's passionate about and, low and behold, vintage music. So, you put in a call to Eric, he needs someone and the handoff occurs. Eric may repay the favor one day.

- Screen on the fly – Hit a mall or strip center and go shopping—for people. The best screening process is to see the realities of behavior and attitude when the candidate is not suspecting it. But here's the trick—if someone is not attentive, it may be the culture of the organization she's in. Walk up to people and start talking to them. What you are looking for is outgoingness, a willingness to converse and communicate and an ability to engage. These are the prequalifiers. The rest you can vet out in the interview.

- Looking for fit – When recruiting for a new employee, it's important to know exactly who it is you are looking for. There are three critical components that must be considered:

  - Fit – Will this person fit in nicely with my team? There will always be the potential of disagreement and dysfunction. Self-intendedness will see to that. And I absolutely encourage having someone who can rattle the cage a little bit; someone who can challenge the big guns and get the existing team to step it up. But, try to avoid hiring an island.

  - Diversity – What void exists on the sales floor? Do you need a bilingual person, a male or female, youth or maturity, blank slate or life experienced?

  - Stepping up – Are you trying to replace the person who was just released or trying to find a twin to the best you have. Don't get caught up in the idea that just because Fred is gone, that you need to replace Fred. Which employee represents a great majority of the attributes and qualities you find most important. That's who you're looking for. Don't try to replace Fred; duplicate Mary.

Interviewing for Passion

First off, you will absolutely have at least two interviews with everyone. And I mean it. No matter how desperate you are and how fabulous he seems, you must do two interviews. The reasons are this:

1. The first interview is the job qualifier. This is used to validate the application details and learn about the applicant's skills and considerations for past jobs.

2. The second interview is where you find out about the person. This is also the place where the realities of working for you are revealed and discussed. But the most important reason for the second interview is the person becomes more comfortable with you and will open up more.

So what do you want to hear come out of your candidate's mouth when you start asking questions? It may not be what they say, but how they are saying it that becomes most important. Let's be real here, a person looking for a gig is going to be well rehearsed. And because the qualifications to work in retail don't necessitate an apprenticeship, a certification or degree or any significant technical skill or knowledge (other than technical or complicated product lines), there's not much the interviewer can use to disqualify a person. So what is a retail street fighter looking for in a salesperson? Let's get the obvious out of the way:

• The first rule of interviewing. Don't try to come off as a big shot or aloof or so important. You want to be friendly and engaging. Ask a ton of questions. Give the applicant the impression that the two of you are totally clicking. This approach is very disarming. It causes the applicant to drop the script and give you more of who she really is.

• Read the application; don't just provide one because you have it. Read it, thoroughly. Did he actually fill it out completely? Is any information missing? Are there time voids between jobs? Did he put his mother as a reference? The time a person takes to fill out an application says a lot about their attention to detail and what is being advertised about his qualifications. However, appreciate that some candidates that have spent the day filling out applications may be burnt on it; so don't totally dismiss it if you feel he didn't take the time to be thorough. Just be prepared to inquire about it.

- Ask the basic questions upfront. Get her talking about herself, her previous jobs, what she liked and disliked and her point of view on supervision style. The more she's talking, the quicker the ramp up time for her to reveal her true self. What is most important here, other than validating the application or résumé, is finding out what she disliked most about previous jobs. You want to make sure it doesn't describe your company or your management style.

If after completing the first interview you decide to bring the person back for a second interview, ask the candidate to mystery shop your store and your primary competitors (unless she's currently working for one of them). I can't believe how many retailers don't do this. This is free mystery shopping!

The questions you should be asking:

In the second interview, the goal is get a feel for their belief system and how the applicant feels about serving another person as a way to make a living. Other than complicated or highly technical product lines or industry specific operational processes that might rule a person out based on ramp up time, there's not a lot to learn when it comes to selling in retail. Don't get me wrong, I love this industry. But I'm honest about what it takes to be successful in it. I have friends who are professionals with four-+ year degrees that make less money than some salespeople I know. To break it down:

- Operations – piece of cake.

- Product knowledge – a couple of weeks with a rep and playing with stuff and it's done.

- Salesmanship – we've all had a rookie out sell a big book just on passion; so this shouldn't require a lot of work.

Plus the ramp up time with salesmanship is more about knowing how to build a bigger ticket and establishing a book of personal trade than anything else. But even rookies can sell the main item quite easily these days.

So what should the street fighter be asking and looking for? You're looking for another street fighter. I like to call these associates "scrappy". What I'm looking to see or sense in the applicant during the second interview is:

- They're outgoing and personable.

- They're engaging and charming.

- They have a sense of competition and drive.

- They can calmly handle conflict. Retail customers are easily riled up. Will the applicant know what to do?

- I want to know they're listening. This is only detectable if you're listening. Do their answers match the question?

So here are the seven questions I always ask:
- **"What are you passionate about?"** This not only lets me know if they are passionate about something, but I'll use it as a metaphor during training. This should also get them to perk up. If the applicant can't muster up some enthusiasm about something he claims to be passionate about, this'll be a problem.

- **"Tell me something unique about yourself."** This takes them off their script and reveals more of who they are. If he continues to tell you about being a people person or previous achievements on the job, remind him that you said "unique". Everyone is a people person!

- **"Did you ever have a customer just go off on you? How did you handle it?"** This will provide you with a gauge of their ability to stay calm. Now if you really want to have some fun with this, get your home video camera and have the staff act out three to six of the worse customer blow ups ever. Play it for the candidate and ask him to comment on it.

- **"What kind of customer are you?"** The applicant's point of view on how she likes to be served when shopping will often be reflected in the way she serves. Have you ever had a salesperson say during a coaching session, "Well I know I don't like it when salespeople are pushy!" This is a window to their beliefs and you just cracked it open.

- **"Do you buy stuff on the Internet? Why?"** I'm setting the stage here to ensure I'm not hiring a human product knowledge kiosk. I don't care if he's purchased stuff on the Internet. I just want to start making a dent in his belief system.

- **"Interview me as your next potential boss."** I look at it this way; he should be just as curious about me as a boss as I am about him as an employee. If the applicant can't come up with one question about my management style, my goals and aspirations, my point of view on something…then this guy will work for anyone and that's a concern for me. I have a thoughtfulness about the kind of person working for me, shouldn't he as well?

- **"Wanna know what its like to work here?"** This is where you get to lay it all on the line. Talk about life with you. Define your expectations for service and performance. Talk about base contribution rates. Review the beliefs and disciplines and ask him for feedback about it. Tell the applicant about scrimmaging and if you want, scrimmage a simple scenario. The idea is to set the stage and possibly scare the tar out of him. If you never hear from him again, that's fine—you'll be better off in the long run. And if you have the guts, tell him to talk to the staff before he leaves. Tell him to feel free to ask them anything. If you are consistent, the staff will reflect it.

Training for Passion

The first 14 days is the sweet spot for both of you. This is where the associate is most open and impressionable. It's also when he gets to see if you were just shoveling it when you defined the expectations of the job. Here's what every retail street fighter should do when on-boarding a new employee:

- Get your operations training out of the way. Have the associate spend a couple of days in each position in the company to develop empathy for the people in that job and to connect the dots for how particles move through the company.

- Handle basic policy violations at the hint of it. If you let the slightest policy violation slip by without addressing it directly, you are opening the door for chasing compliance issues. Here's the script:

"Hi Bob. I noticed you were 10 minutes late today."

"Yeah, sorry about that, I had to drop some gas in my car."

"So is this going to be a problem going forward?"

"Well…it shouldn't be."

"Good, because if you think it will be we can save some time here and call it a day."

"Wow, I'm sorry Arnie. I didn't realize it was that big of a deal."

"I understand that. If you want, you can talk to Gary about it."

"Gary? I heard Gary was let go just before I got here."

"Exactly."

If you address policy violations up front like that, then in no time, you will be only addressing how to sell more, which are the conversations everybody likes having.

- Scrimmage everyday for 14 days. This kind of consistency will get the associate used to the idea that its part of the job and it's going to happen.

- Keep the propaganda machine in high gear and get the staff involved in it.

Once past the orientation period, the retail street fighter has to sustain performance in this salesperson. This is an ongoing campaign. Once you cut'em loose, self-intendedness will begin to creep in. There are many cases of people who start working from home and cannot stay focused and productive. Sustaining performance is a communication issue. It's all about ensuring the staff is constantly immersed in your cause.

Foundationally speaking, there are plenty of tools available that help in the orientation of new employees, and if you want to know more about that, please feel free to contact me. I've had the pleasure of working for some of the greatest HR people in retail. Some are available to me to help develop customer learning platforms. To make the employee experience superb, the retail street fighter should have tools like job descriptions, daily training regiments, tests and quizzes, and video/audio training programs as core components for the ongoing development of the staff. And then when the honeymoon has passed, the orientation has completed and the associate has been absorbed into the fabric of the company, the only thing left is how we keep her inspired and striving for more.

In one sense I could say to go back to the beginning of the book because essentially this comes full circle. As mentioned in the beginning of this chapter, the employee experience is about creating and maintaining a work environment that defines expectations, has fun, provides objective and developmental feedback, and thus it fuels the spirit of the employee to reciprocate by paying those experiences forward to the customer. This book is about that.

And if everything you read in this book seems too involved and complicated for you, well you can always wing it. But trust me when I tell you, the giants of retail never sleep. Regardless of the category they just killed, these guys are always planning their consumption of the customer base months and sometimes years in advance. You may think you are too small to rumble on this street and they would never pick on you. Mrs. Ritterbush has been shopping in your store since 1985 and may always be loyal to your store and you're fine with that.

But if you suspect your customer based is shrinking or minimally has stopped growing (which means its shrinking), then chug down a couple of raw eggs, hit the street running, and know that its not the size of the retailer that matters, it's the depth of the experience.

Biography: Arnold Capitanelli, III

Arnold Capitanelli's career history outlines 20 years of developing and executing successful sales strategies that are based on company growth initiatives and superior customer experiences. He has an extensive background in not only developing customer-centric sales/service models, but has also successfully executed them within several national retail brands.

With a background in sales, retail operations, training and development, strategic development and national account management, Arnie spent the past 20 years building and executing customer-centric selling models. He has worked for Watkins Manufacturing (makers of HotSpring Portable Spas), Manny's Musical Instruments, David's Bridal and After Hours Formalwear as well as provided training and consulting for companies like Ashley Furniture, T-Mobile, and Cardello Lighting and Electrical Supply.

In addition to his business acumen, Arnie is an accomplished and highly energetic speaker and has delivered keynote addresses world wide. Arnie provides insights, techniques and strategies to retailers within any product category on how to grow their businesses and deliver exceptional customer experiences based on his revolutionary concepts of customer advocacy. His seminar "Every Customer Counts" is the freshest information on building Market and Customer Share and addresses "new school" issues with the generation now entering the sales force.

About CAP

Customer Advocate Programs is a retail performance improvement company that creates and implements selling models for companies looking to define their customer experience, create consistency on the sales floor and ultimately improve performance in top and bottom line financials. Customer Advocate Programs provides its clients with the training tools, content and resources necessary to deliver exceptional customer experiences that provides for sustainable growth and profitability.

Overview

Over the past 20 years, Arnold Capitanelli III, President of Customer Advocate Programs, has been specializing in creating fully integrated performance improvement systems as a senior level operator and consultant in several well established retail brands including Manny's Music, David's Bridal, After Hours Formalwear, Cardello Lighting Showrooms and several Ashley Furniture HomeStores.

His work with these brands caused Arnie to develop a retail specific training program called Every Customer Counts. The program is designed to help independent specialty retailers define their customer experience in order to maximize each opportunity and create loyalty to the brand by exceeding customer expectations.

Every Customer Counts is built on a five-pillar concept that focuses a retail organization on customer centric activities that maximizes the potential of each transaction and exposes erosion in the disciplines that define a superior customer experience. Combining real life experience with proven methods for maximizing each transactional opportunity, Arnie blends his program with a company's current business model so that implementation is seamless and non-disruptive to the organization as implementation occurs.

The program is defined as:

1. Foundations for customer centricity: Defining and implementing beliefs systems, organizational disciplines and performance accountabilities that form the foundation for success.

2. The customer experience - made simple: The creation of specific disciplines, techniques and training tools that underlie the customer experience and ensure the store teams can deliver those experiences with each customer.

3. Gap analysis – Minimizing performance erosion: Tracking individual and actionable performance indicators that provide direction on how to improve customer experiences.

4. Being the customer advocate: Developing the skills managers need to have in order to ensure the core values of beliefs, disciplines, awareness and commitment are being demonstrated with every customer interaction.

5. The employee experience: The creation of a learning platform to ensure that anyone who interacts with the customer is representing the company's beliefs and exceeding customer expectations.

The Customer Advocate Philosophy

The Customer Advocate Program was not made for retail; it was born from retail. CAP was created within the walls of a growing retail organization and built on a very simple premise: "Serve the Underserved".

CAP began with the customer in mind. The foundation of the program is steeped with market research and customer feedback. The program identifies the ways an independent retail store can build both Market Penetration (transactions) and Customer Share (average transaction) by capitalizing on critical moments in the customer experience.

The key to CAP's success however lies in the method in which it moves salespeople to behave in a way that exceeds customer expectations and maximizes each customer facing opportunity. CAP is built on these basic tenets:

- Every customer counts. Success in retail begins with an awareness of the importance of every single footprint. In today's marketplace, the presence of a customer in a brick and mortar retail store is not happenstance.
- Salespeople are generally self-intended; they will typically default to behavior based on what they believe is right for them. Therefore, performance management models that lean to the extremes of either high compliance or high camaraderie will not have a long-term effect on behavior. In order to create and sustain behavioral consistency, the associate's core beliefs must be addressed.
- Goal setting should be motivating, inspiring and based on personal levels of achievement. Goal setting is ineffective when used to punish or humiliate. Performance accountability, on the other hand, is based on defined minimum contribution benchmarks. Feedback on individual performance is reserved for performance improvement meetings.
- Gaps in the customer experience are realized in performance trends of actionable metrics. If the associate is not serving or selling the "correct way" it will show up in a statistical trend.

- Training creates short-term compliance. Learning creates long-term behavioral change. The employee experience will shape the customer experience.

CAPabilities

Because most independent retailers tend to have their financial resources tied up in marketing, merchandising, payroll and other operational expenses, the training function often takes a back seat to other pressing expenditures. Thus retail owners and managers are left with trying to find sales associates who appear to have selling skills when they are hired. Unfortunately, this not always the case and managers are left trying to determine how to get the associate to serve the customer "their way". Developing internal training platforms, hiring training staff or contracting outside vendors can be costly.

CAP is very focused on sustainability. This can only occur by making seminars and onsite consultation/training very affordable so retailers can maximize exposure of the programs to the very people responsible for engaging the customer. The goal is to provide workshops, materials, templates, consulting, training and documentation at an extremely affordable price so retailers can afford to send new managers, MITs, assistant managers and provide refresher courses without having to compromise their marketing budget.

Arnie Capitanelli is the primary voice of CAP and never uses contracted trainers to facilitate public or private workshops and seminars. Arnie CAP is also deeply involved with individual consultative projects and only uses consultants with proven track records as high-level retail operators in their respective fields (i.e. financial planning and analysis, human resource development, etc).

Consulting

When working onsite with an independent retailer, customer advocate programs does not rely solely on a seminar-based format and complicated sales-training modules as the means for developing sustainable behaviors and performance improvement. Although there is always a need for company meetings as a way of disseminating information and introducing behavioral change, real sustainable change occurs by working directly in the stores and with company executives and through the development of training materials that define the customer experience. The format relies on:

- Spending time in stores and corporations for the purpose of defining customer expectations and better understand the critical dynamics of the customer experience

- Defining the company's belief system and underlying disciplines that are most likely to maximize Customer Share and Market Penetration

- Developing performance roadmaps that trend gaps in critical performance measurements and identifies behavioral deficiencies

- Creating communication vehicles to ensure the store organization understands, embraces and can manifest the company's brand and service proposition to the customer

- Enhancing employee experiences to create loyalty to the brand, translating to higher levels of service with the customer

- Facilitating real-time "manager scrimmaging" that hones their skills for driving associate self-awareness for behavioral development

- Ensuring that all programs are replicatable and sustainable to ensure consistency throughout the chain

- Developing staffing models for regular and busy day traffic trends
- Providing additional resources for:
  - Human resource development
  - Financial planning and analysis
  - Branding, marketing and community outreach